# THE SCROLLS OF CORNELIUS

## Book 4 in the Seekers Series

### JEFF GAURA

Copyright ©2024 by Jeff Gaura

All rights reserved solely by the author. The author guarantees all contents all contents are original and do not infringe upon the legal rights of any other person or work. No part of this book may be re-produced in any form without the permission of the author. The views expressed in this book are not necessarily those of the publisher.

ISBN: 978-1-961879-58-4 (Paperback)
ISBN: 978-1-961879-59-1 (Ebook)

Printed in the United States of America

# Foreword

During the summer of 2021, I lay by the pool in my backyard, enjoying the beautiful scenery and all the wildlife in the woods and trees that surround our property. Of course, I could not stop wondering what Eliza, Caleb, Yael, Dor, Benji, and old Domitian were doing. I smiled a lot but I also had a few sad moments as I began to create a timeline of events that might reignite the hearts of my readers. It took one or two of those poolside moments before I had a new folder in my computer, and Word Documents magically appeared in it. Before I knew what happened, my train came off the track and by the end of the year, I had written five more books. Disciples were created. Some conflict was initiated and brought to a crescendo, and transitions occurred as characters aged out. The Roman Empire expanded; history said it did. So did the Church; and they continued to cross paths both in downtown Rome and on the fringes of new places as far away as Afghanistan and England. Commerce changed, greed and lust flourished, and there always remained a loyal remnant on both sides who struggled to take the best of the past and apply it to the future.

The issues of first-century Roman and Palestine and the vast array of documentation on that timeline were intriguing, and drama was in everything I read. Even though they existed exclusively on paper, my actors were young and had much life left in them. I decided to wake them up and see where they might go! In the North Carolina heat, I created a vision for a new series of five books, and I tacked onto the prophecy that I started in the first trilogy and created some new foreshadowing.

My starting point for continuing the story was a fundamental tenant of humanity: we are enthralled by a good story. Seldom, though, do we get the whole story. We normally hear the time frame's action, adventure, and perhaps a few embellishments. The part of the story that leads up to that moment and all that happens afterward rarely, if ever, make it to the stories we remember. To say it differently, I drive close to 200,000 miles between car accidents. No one seems to care about what happens as I am driving and not wrecking my car. That is the human condition, and historical fiction is the playground for those who know this.

In the days of the New Testament, Rome ruled the world. One in every four people lived and died under Roman law, from England to Africa and Syria to Spain. The Emperor and the Senate governed the Empire. Discussing the times of Christ without reference to Rome is like describing an apple pie without reference to the crust. History shows the players crossing into each other's spaces all the time. Therefore, I decided that I should, too.

But Rome was much more than just one city. It was an empire with a vast collection of states and cultures backed up by a powerful military, a single language of commerce, and a single rule of law. Even allowing for an occasional revolt, the empire was an enormous achievement. It served as a great marketplace for its citizens and remnants of its impact are alive; after all, Amazon.com is fashioned in the image of the Roman Empire!

The upsides would make a modern millennial salivate. Travel and trade were unhindered, unlike any time in world history. There were no passports, visas, gun restrictions, mask restrictions, taxes on Bitcoin, or vaccination requirements. Do you want to go somewhere and do something? Get on a boat. Get on a horse. Walk. Limitations were time and money, just like today; but after that, you could "be" and see how it worked. You might need to sell yourself into slavery for a year or two, but what the heck? It might be worth it.

Some downsides needed to be inseparable from the storyline. There were no fundamental human rights, as humans were possessions, often worth less than a horse or a cow taken to market for sale. Women adopted the social status of their families and could not do something independently to move up. Marriage relationships were much like those in Game of Thrones. Who you married determined the security and social status of the next generation.

I specifically found the story of Cornelius the Centurion to be one that was chock full of unanswered questions. His now-deceased son was at the core of my last trilogy, so why not make future descendants who struggled with the same opposing worldviews central to this series? His history and position in the Roman military and the Christian church had me begging for more available knowledge. The biblical tale occupies less than a page of Chapter 10 in the Book of Acts. Cornelius is often credited with being the first Gentile to experience the Holy Spirit, but we don't know that. Cities around the world are named after him but here in the US, we have no cities named after Nero, even though he was his boss and had a lot more power than Cornelius. There was just something about this guy.

What we are not taught in church is that Cornelius was one of the most powerful and unencumbered men in the Roman Empire. For practical purposes, he lived on the other side of the moon from those who oversaw his day-to-day actions. If there was a person in the empire who could "go rogue" and get away with disappearing for a year, Cornelius was the guy. To be clear, Cornelius was a centurion, meaning he was responsible for over 100 soldiers and the funding from Rome's coffers to act as the battering ram of the Roman Empire in the province of Manasseh. Roman called all of Israel "Judah", but it soon adopted a guttural and disgusting name of Palestine, and the people from there were called Palestina, a most insulting name.

As a centurion, he served as chief of police and doubled as the magistrate, hearing all cases that required justice. In the modern world, the executive and judicial branches are often considered to be in conflict and kept separate, but no such silliness existed in ancient Rome. In addition to his responsibilities, he was the head of all the tax collectors. I can only imagine what it would be like if he were alive today. One man would decide abortion rights, gun control, voting precincts, COVID reactions, prescription laws, insider trading rules, and election results. It would never fly. Yet back then, it did. And this one man was called honorable as he danced between the heart of Christ and the enforcement of Roman law without playing favorites.

Under Cornelius, Caesarea's population grew by some estimates to over 100,000 people, and it was a transit point for merchants from around the world. His day job was administering that city. The Bible doesn't talk about any of that. It must be neither interesting nor important. That makes it kind of like my 200,000 miles of driving without a wreck.

This fictional sequence traverses a few moments in the generations of lives connected to one of the more powerful men in the Roman Empire. My mind has run circles around what he experienced before and after this brief encounter with Simon Peter and the Holy Spirit. I wish the Book of Acts were a lot longer. At the least, I wish it contained more "the day after Simon Peter left Caesarea" commentaries.

Another part left out of church commentary was the many capital projects in play at that time. Rome was building connections to the Silk Road and the Jerusalem highway. There was also a vast aqueduct project, all during the time Cornelius was in charge. Simon Peter's arrival, escorted in by the Holy Spirit, happened during a time when migrant workers and ethnic conflict were occupying Cornelius' staff. He was putting people to death every day of the week. Those had to be a part of my story.

As a new follower of Christ, he had to manage all of it. He obviously did, as the aqueducts are still in place today and the remains of the highways are all over the place. Yet he assuredly struggled with appeasing his financial ledgers and his orgy-hungry boss now that he had a personal savior.

This complicated background made me wonder. Can you imagine sentencing men to death by crucifixion after learning that your savior died via crucifixion as part of the forgiveness of sins? From what I can glean from history, he did it several hundred times. I can't understand that, no matter how much I read.

I have decided to spend these months placing myself in his shoes and writing about it. This book sets the stage for one of the most inspirational men in early church history. And by definition, it is rich in sadness and traumatic loss. Pull up your pants. This is the world of Cornelius, like it or not.

# Introduction to Cornelius

The name "Cornelius" comes from the Latin word "cornu", meaning "horn".

His father named him Cornelius after the famous Roman Cornelius Skippio who defeated Hannibal the Barbarian, thus crushing the empire of Carthage. Skippio's legacy is a part of every Roman citizen's education and his generational image of leadership under duress convinced his father that his firstborn would bear his name.

As a young man, Cornelius proved himself to be athletic and intelligent. As such, he met the requirements to join the elite guard of the Roman military at age 16. His family delivered him to the capital city's recruiting center, the same place his father enlisted some 25 years earlier. After ceremonially saying goodbye to his family, he entered basic training and was soon shipped to Gaul for his first assignment. He was large by Roman military standards and he stood a full head higher than almost everyone. He was stationed in Gaul and made a comfortable life until he was 19. He quickly learned the local language and was found to be invaluable as he negotiated and traded for food and supplies during their stay. Yet he also connected with the people. He often played with the local children; he found them to be most forgiving as he practiced his language skills, and the children loved playing with a man taller than anyone they had encountered.

Leadership in Rome learned of his language skills and he rapidly received field advancements to become a squad leader or decurion before turning 18. After he returned from his assignment in Gaul, his parents arranged for him to marry Valentina, a girl from a well-to-do family of healers who lived outside of Rome. The newlyweds stayed with Cornelius' family for less than a month before

Cornelius received a new assignment on the island nation of Crete. Since they were now married, Valentina was allowed to travel with her husband on what was considered an administrative assignment. Val quickly became friends with two women whose husbands were also in Cornelius' regiment. She also spent time each morning doing odd jobs for some of the merchants on the docks where her husband was most busy with the affairs of Rome. She became his one-person reconnaissance team and she kept him abreast of the affairs of the commoner.

At first, Cornelius thought the regiment's new mission was unimportant and he felt it wasteful to put well-trained fighting men in charge of commerce management and taxation. However, his wife convinced him to table his complaints and focus on working hard, as if he thought his work was inappropriate for a man of his talents. His wife used their extra pay from having an overseas assignment to hire twin Egyptian girls to help with housework. They let the two girls live in the extra room in their house. The girls ate with them and would go shopping in the markets with them; that exposure facilitated Corn and Val's learning of their language and a doorway into understanding Egyptian culture.

Corn's language skills did not stop with Greek, Latin, Gaelic, and Egyptian. He also took to the language of commerce and could settle disputes between Egyptians, Carthaginians, Gauls, Greeks, and Ebreet without using his blade. At least that was the story he told his wife after he came home and she asked how his day had gone.

He was considered economically creative. With input from his men, he devised a lighting system using whale oil lanterns that he thought would deter crime on the docks at night when reports of incidents were the highest. He gave tax credits to any merchant who would provide fuel and burn a lantern all night long on the docks near where they were moored. Soon, every merchant in the harbor lit up the night and the lack of shadows caused the crime rates to fall to an all-time low since Rome began tracking them. Cornelius needed fewer men working late nights patrolling the area, which saved Rome money. Merchants were excited to pay less in tariffs than any other Mediterranean port. Soon other boats began using Crete as their preferred port of call, as it was now affordable to smaller sailing companies and individual proprietors. Cornelius kept his balance sheet as lean as possible so he didn't have to explain his choices and the resulting benefits. The combined strategy of offering tax credits and keeping the reporting as small as possible worked. His Legate read his weekly and monthly financial reports of this success and promoted him. He instructed Cornelius to act as a magistrate in the Cretan courts while their centurion was inland working on other affairs. Little did Cornelius know that his Legate knew that a position in Caesarea was soon available. He had Cornelius in mind to become the Optio or second in command of the regiment.

With that promotion, Cornelius became the highest-ranking teenager in Rome's military history. Rome was preparing to undertake several large construction projects in Caesarea. They needed a man who could be there for several decades to ensure stability for the duration of the construction. Nero himself read Cornelius' report and balance sheets regarding Crete and he listened as his Legate told him about his strategy with whale oil and tariffs. Nero saw an ambition in Cornelius that reminded him of Augustus and he told the Legate that he would personally promote him to Optio. After Cornelius arrived at his promotion ceremony, it was recorded that Nero told the senate that Cornelius had the right traits to develop the economy in the outlying province of Judah. The Senate agreed and he was fast-tracked into a leadership role that would keep him two weeks away from Rome for several decades.

Neither Nero, the Senate, nor Cornelius could fathom the depth of God's plans. He would use Cornelius to become one of the first gentiles to experience the gifts of the Holy Spirit and his offspring and students would carry the message of a risen Messiah to all the corners of the world. God went to the top of the military while He picked Cornelius as the first military leader called into the service of a risen Messiah. His adopted offspring became rabbis, warriors, businessmen, parents, a Roman Senator, and a minister, one step below the emperor.

Cornelius' life story shows a deep need for a Messiah that no one alive in the 21$^{st}$ century can understand. He lost his son to overzealous Roman soldiers. His only daughter married and moved off. As his days neared their end, he decided to give his estate to an adopted nephew and nearly all his wealth to his Ebreet servants at his estate in the hills above Caesarea. His nephew appeared to have all the right characteristics to become his replacement and Cornelius invited him to come and live with him and receive more training.

He died long before Caleb completed all his training. Against Roman tradition, he asked to be buried and not cremated. He left hundreds of journal entries detailing his struggles to reconcile Rome's demands with those of a risen Messiah.

This part of Cornelius' story does not appear in the Bible or Roman history books. It is the tale of his deep sorrows and heartfelt loss as he acted as the battering arm of the most potent and heathenistic force that the world has ever known, all the while trying to live for a man killed on a cross at nearly the same time he was being birthed in luxury.

# Cast of Characters:

**Cornelius Antiochus: Centurion of Caesarea.** Biblical character from the Book of Acts, Chapter 10. Although he was promoted to the rank of Tribune, he and his family continued to use the title centurion till his death. He was buried with the centurion insignia.

**Valentina Antiochus: wife of Cornelius.** She experienced the Holy Spirit as a young girl but didn't know it. God planted her in Cornelius' life to be his helpmate. In the end, she changed at least as many lives as he did, but she never received any credit for her efforts.

**Eliza Antiochus:** Ebreet girl from Naphtali who led Emperor Titus to Christ a few days before he mysteriously died. A linguistically skilled and trained rabbi in the Christian tradition. Yet she was a merchant and economist at her core. Timid and weak, she was one of the greatest female leaders in Judean history - possessor of the spiritual gift of healing as well as teaching and discipleship.

**Yael:** An Ebreet slave whose freedom was paid for by Eliza after Caleb won a gladiator battle in the Coliseum. She became Caleb's wife and mother to Mishi and John Marcus. Eliza's parents adopted her. Eliza refers to her as "sister". Bold in character yet also a peacemaker, she was an ultra-fast learner and insightful Torah instructor. She was a lifetime homemaker to a centurion who struggled deeply with the disconnect between what his God wanted and what his employer wanted.

**Caleb:** Yael's loyal husband and Cornelius' replacement as Centurion of Caesarea. Son of Yael and Mishi, the first two people to make copies of the Book of Luke and Acts. His mother and father were Rabbis in the Ebreet/Christian tradition but were killed by Roman soldiers when Caleb was 16. He passed Cornelius to become the youngest centurion in the history of the Roman empire, and on a first-name basis with three emperors. He fought in the most famous venues in the Roman Empire: the Coliseum and Circus Maximus. His victories were categorically epic and his name was renowned within the leadership of the Senate. His public relationship with emperors Titus, Domitian, and Trajan is the stuff of history.

**Katya:** Eliza's biological mother and Yael's adopted mother. She also adopts all of Eliza's disciples and becomes their mother - Eliza's most important counselor. She is level-headed and leads a life of gratitude. She birthed two children, 18 years apart.

**Dor:** Rabbi who called Eliza. He is a former soldier who operates the House of Healing in Gaza, a facility focused on helping people through trauma and recovery from the impacts of the Roman Empire's expansion.

**Ebreet:** Anyone of Hebrew or Jewish heritage.

**Palestina:** Roman name meant as a derogatory slur used to describe anyone from the area currently known as Israel, Gaza, Lebanon, and Northeast Egypt.

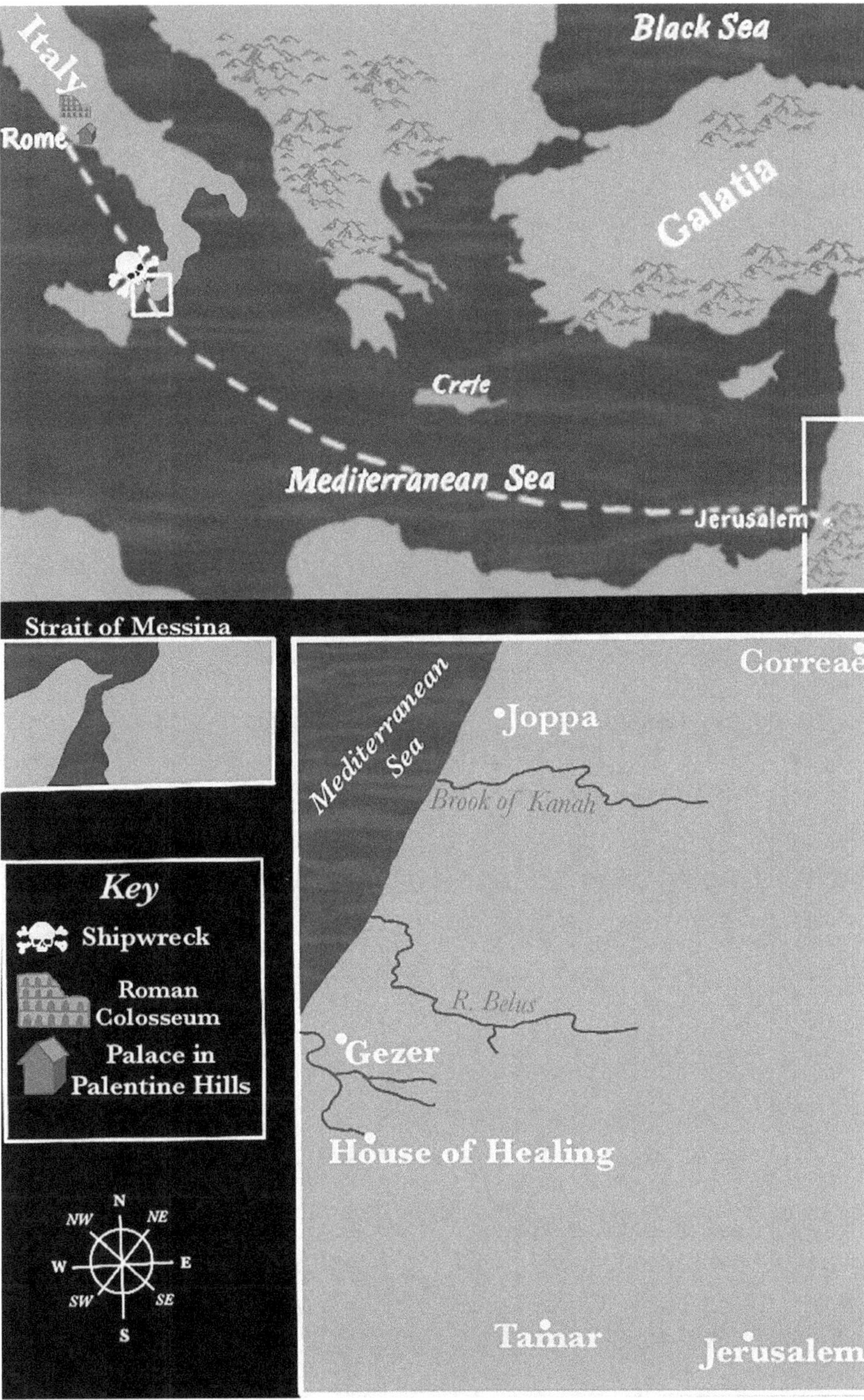

Italy
Rome
Black Sea
Galatia
Crete
Mediterranean Sea
Jerusalem
Strait of Messina
Mediterranean Sea
Correaë
Joppa
Brook of Kanah
R. Belus
Gezer
House of Healing
Key
Shipwreck
Roman Colosseum
Palace in Palentine Hills
N
NW
NE
W
E
SW
SE
S
Tamar
Jerusalem

# Chapter 1:
# First Day in Court

Today was Caleb's first day in his new job as magistrate of Caesarea, a city of more than 100,000. His uncle Cornelius was now retired and Caesarea was Caleb's to govern. Uncle Cornelius had trained the young man to be a fair and impartial judge and Caleb had sat next to his uncle something like 50 times as he watched the old man cast judgment. Sometimes, it was over a loaf of stolen bread. Other times, it was robbery and murder. Cornelius was not with him today, and Caleb was feeling excited and a bit nervous. He didn't read any of the reports about the crimes these men had been charged with; he would do that as he listened to them and learned about their character.

He had already decided to make some changes to his uncle's way of governance. The first one was perhaps the riskiest move of his short career to date. He decided to bring his wife, Yael, and their toddler, Mishi, to the place he held court, a semi-circle by the sea. He didn't need her for long but needed her for impact at the start. His uncle told him not to include her, and he used some vulgar language to make his point. He and Cornelius eventually agreed to disagree on this matter. Caleb agreed that she needed to leave and be out of visual and auditory range before he beheaded or crucified anyone. Cornelius was adamant that he would not let her see any of that, threatening to circumcise Caleb a second time if Yael came home upset at what she saw. Cornelius could speak to Caleb like that as the two of them were the highest-ranking members of the Roman army in this part of the world. Caleb also knew that Cornelius loved him like a son.

"She is more important than gold," the old man would tell Caleb in his softer moments.

"I don't care if you become the emperor or sleep in his house. She will still outrank you in matters of the home and the heart. Get used to that," he would say.

"Your job requires that you kill folks now and then. She doesn't need to see that or hear you talk about it. She needs to be the mother of your children and the woman who makes your house into a home. She doesn't need to be a part of any bloodletting; keep her the hell out of there."

Caleb and Yael lived with Cornelius and his wife Valentina, and he was grateful for their offer to live with them right after they got married. They called them "uncle" and "aunt", but they were more like parents than relatives. Yael's mother died before she became a slave and her father was not a productive member of society. Caleb's parents were celebrity rabbis and the Roman Army killed them upon learning that they were teaching about a God other than the emperor. Caleb and Yael knew that they were more indebted to Cornelius than they could express.

"Tell me how things go tomorrow in court. And don't lie to me." Those were the last words Cornelius said to Caleb as he laid down for bed last night. Yael watched the two of them as he gave the young man last-minute pointers on how to run the court and reiterated his disdain for Caleb including Yael in his court.

"Corn is just trying to protect you and keep Caleb from going insane," Valentina told Yael as the two of them separated. Valentina mentored Yael as much as Cornelius mentored Caleb. Yael had learned that Cornelius meant well, but he was always so abrasive with Caleb that it upset Yael. She knew she didn't want her husband to use that same language with their children.

Caleb knew his day as magistrate was coming when he and his wife started their mentorship under Cornelius and Valentina about three years ago. His senior lieutenants knew his plan, but neither the soldiers nor the scribes and sentries in attendance knew what Caleb was about to do. He was the new Centurion, adept with a blade, and the best archer of any from the tribe of Benjamin. Most knew little more than that. The next morning came early and Caleb and Yael prepared to go long before sunrise. They had a moment together before she would go and wake up their baby. Their servants had already prepared tea for all the men on trial and Yael had a change of clothing with her. She was excited about her husband and supportive of him.

"You finally get to sign your name on everything!" said Yael.

"I know," Caleb said, wearing a big smile. Yael looked fondly at her husband, picking up the royal stamp of the centurion and attaching it to his belt next to his sword. He knew that at the end of today's events, he would seal the record of his rulings for the first time with his seal, not his uncle's seal. Today would be his day to record Roman history, not a shared one. Today, he set his uncle's legacy aside and started his own. And Yael lifted her man as she uniquely could do.

"I love you, Caleb. Kiss me," she said, pulling on this forearm to kiss her. Once he pulled back, he looked her in the eye.

"Helper?" he said, reaching out his hand. His wife interlocked her fingers in his and held the torch they would use to navigate in her other hand, and they started down the stairs of their compound toward the heart of Caesarea. His mother was a legendary Torah teacher and he had heard her preach to many that wives are meant to be "helpers equal to men". For Caleb, that meant Yael needed to be there. That was his argument though Cornelius didn't agree with it.

"You look very nice in your uniform, despite this light," she said. She knew Caleb needed that kind of affirmation. He didn't say anything that signaled Yael that her words meant the world to him, but she knew her husband. Caleb was feeling pride with the insignia of the Centurion on his lapel. He had not worn it before and she needed to acknowledge that; ironically, she sewed the insignia on his uniform over a month ago when Cornelius announced his last day of work. He wore the uniform in the house one time but this was the first instance of wearing his new rank in public.

Caleb had plenty of time to think as they walked to court in the pre-dawn. Caleb had sat through enough late-night wine bottles with his uncle to know that crime was a growing problem in Caesarea. The Roman senate and the supporting merchant class had commissioned a series of new roads from Caesarea, one to Jerusalem, and another northeast towards the Silk Road. Caleb and Cornelius worked together to create and administer a toll system to finance the upkeep. As was to be expected, the Senate wished the tolls to be a revenue source and the merchants thought that tolls would create a barrier to good business. As part of his final journey to Rome, Cornelius and Caleb met with leaders of the Senate. They negotiated a tariff collection mechanism that everyone agreed would be fair and easy to administer. The bridges were the easiest places to levy a use tax, as travelers lacked any alternative routes to get their wagons across the rivers. Caleb watched as Cornelius defended the merchants, petitioning for no tariffs to use these new roads leaving Caesarea. The leaders of the Senate agreed over dinner and more wine that there was already ample income from the port traffic and there was no need to incite resentment from the merchant class by adding to their cost of doing business. Leaving Caesarea should be free. The roads to get there would be where they made their money.

And with these new tariffs and additional traffic came new crimes and criminals. Caleb decided to use his first day as Centurion and magistrate to ensure that he would protect the merchant class' interests as much as he protected Rome's. That shared purpose Cornelius agreed with. His vision was to educate the community that anyone who attempted to interrupt fair and honest commerce would be punished. He decided that it was the centurion's job to dispose of those who cheated registered merchants of economic progress and Caleb had a place and a plan to do this.

He and Yael arrived, affectionately holding hands. Yale knew that when Caleb was scared or nervous, he would lean on her stability and would treat her like a queen. They were a team in this, whereas Cornelius tried to do all centurion-related tasks by himself. Yael's servants accompanied them and they carried clay pots of hot tea and two backpacks full of bread they had prepared in the early morning. Once they arrived in court, she gave all but one of her servants the rest of the day off, handing each one a week's wage in coin to spend in the market and enjoy themselves for their middle-of-the-night shift making tea and bread. Yael promised to find them and join them mid-morning, but she had one job to do with her husband.

"Is everything ready?" Caleb asked one of his lieutenants. He and his men knew the protocol at the seaside court of justice.

"Yes, Centurion," the soldier said. Caleb expected 50 or so arrestees shackled together outside in a line and awaiting trial. The men could be heard talking a bit and there was some torchlight, so he could see that it was the typical mix of people and cultures.

He didn't expect any city residents to be in attendance to watch "the new guy" serve Roman justice. He didn't care who watched him, anyway. His uncle taught him that the most important audience was the Messiah; one day, he would stand judgment before him. That thought was always sobering, no matter how many times Uncle Cornelius reminded him of it. There would be no deferments until tomorrow. For these 50 men, court started and ended today, regardless of circumstance.

Looking out at the harbor, architecture and quality of roads made it obvious that Roman leadership and politicians had invested a lot of time and money to make the port city of Caesarea a trading center second to none on the empire's eastern edge. Safer than the lands around Antioch, Corinth, or Carthage, Caesarea was the ideal port to build a gateway east to Kushun. Caleb's Legate told him that the empire would eventually expand to China, and his city was a key part of that expansion.

The redness of the winter sunrise was now greeting the warmer air coming off the Mediterranean Sea to the West. They entered the open-air semi-circle that served as a Roman court. It sat on the edge of the sea, a short walk south of the port operations center. Everyone charged with a crime during the last week now stood in the cold and waited at one of two entrances to the semi-circle. Each arrestee knew that there were two outcomes of any Roman court in an outpost more than a few days from the heart of the empire. On this day, everyone would either be found innocent or guilty and for many of the 50, guilty would mean the death sentence.

Since the first person's trial had not yet commenced, the Roman soldiers did what they always did before court started. They all sipped hot tea and ate warm bread that Yael's servants made. A few soldiers held the prisoners in line at the northside entrance, releasing them from the iron clasps on their ankles and wrists one at a time when it was their turn for trial. Once their case was heard, they would exit to the south and whatever life awaited them.

Caleb took his place on a stone chair covered with luxurious pillows at the center of the outdoor semi-circle, and it was here that he would listen to each man's story. He took off his helmet, loosened the straps on his sandals, and removed his bracers and gauntlets. He kept his two-edged gladius in front of him, unsheathed, for all on trial to see. After all, it was possible that he would personally administer justice if the situation warranted it. Although he prayed that he would not have to decapitate a man with his wife watching, he knew it was possible. She knew to close her eyes and cover her ears if she saw him pick up his sword. To his left, on a smaller table, sat two scribes. Their job was to record all spoken claims on parchment. Each man recorded an independent account of what happened. Then a third man compared the copies, ensuring that the details matched before one copy would be sent back to Rome. The other stayed in the Hall of Records in Caesarea. Before Caleb was born, Cornelius decided that all criminal proceedings were public records; if anyone wanted to know what happened when someone failed to return from court, they could read for themselves.

Caleb assigned three fully armed soldiers at each entranceway as his uncle did. One held his unsheathed gladius while the other two spoke and answered questions. No Roman soldier could converse with anyone other than another Roman citizen or soldier while his sword was in his hand. History taught that words provoke a sword strike more than an aggressive action, and the Centurion in charge commanded all who held their weapons to avoid speaking lest they lose their tongue.

Caleb made a single motion to the guards at the north entrance and the proceedings began.

The first man was brought before the dais and he appeared to be in the prime of his life, but he lacked legal representation. Caleb's men had offered it to him last night, as was the Roman custom, but the man refused. After removing all the shackles, the man began speaking without prompting.

"Honorable Centurion, let me explain," the man spoke as he started his plea. Caleb raised his hand to interrupt and the soldier beside the man elbowed the accused to ensure he understood not to speak further.

"First things first. You are in the land of the tribe of Manasseh and we will follow the customs of this place before we start your trial," he said. He gestured for what appeared to be a female Ebreet servant to pour a cup of warm tea and she humbly carried it to the accused man. The man took the cup from her without looking and attempted to speak again, but Caleb raised his hand again.

"First drink!" No one spoke after Caleb issued the command. The prisoner also didn't wait. He put the cup to his mouth and took a sip. He nodded up and down, saying that it tasted good, but he looked at no one when he did it. The slave stood next to him, staring down while holding the teapot in case he wanted more.

Caleb knew the man was cold and would value the warm beverage once he let himself. Caleb had seen how the men who came before the court could ignore hunger and thirst when their lives and livelihoods were in jeopardy. He also knew that many in line had not slept the previous night and would be fatigued before the trial started. This man nodded and put the cup to his lips again. The warm liquid was calming him, just as Caleb had hoped.

While he drank, Caleb took a moment to look at their surroundings. Immediately next to the location of this judgment seat was the terminus of the monumental aqueduct that had just been completed before Cornelius retired. The labor required to construct the aqueduct and the two new roadways most likely brought all those standing accused to this city in the first place. These projects took nearly ten years to complete and the efforts employed thousands of men. Caleb admired the stone towers that held the water above the city. They were auspicious. Fresh and clean drinking water now continuously flowed from the Golan Heights to Caesarea. Caleb had already heard reports from the physicians of decreased illness in all parts of the city. Valentina's parents were physicians and she took ownership of making sure Caleb and Yael knew the importance of monitoring the health of the people they now governed. Valentina had mentored Yael, introducing her to all the local physicians. These relationships taught her how to gauge the levels of disease and pestilence in the Caesarea district. Yael became Caleb's barometer of health and success.

Among the accused were men from Galilee to the north and Judah and Gaza to the south, and there were men from the Roman province of Philippi. However, many were black-as-the-night Egyptians from the Negev and several of the larger, stronger, dark-brown Philistines. There were a few pale-skinned Gauls, but they followed the rules and seldom found themselves on trial.

Caleb studied the man's body language as he finished drinking his tea. He looked at the other men in line, knowing this man's outcome would be seen by everyone else and would change the flow of the rest of the day's proceedings.

"My wife and her servants made that tea this morning," said Caleb, using a friendly tone that he might use with a family member. The man on trial gave no response. The cups were small and the accused gestured to the slave girl to refill his cup. The slave girl respectfully filled up his cup and awaited him to finish. Once he finished the second cup, the girl walked away and Caleb began the trial.

"The records before me state that you took something and didn't pay for it; is that correct?"

Caleb knew better than to use solely the report's contents to engage an arrested man. He sought to know if the man was aware of what he was accused of or if he was in denial of his crime. Although his questions required a "yes/no" answer, Caleb knew that most men would offer more details. Above all else, Caleb always hoped the men before him would take the path of humility ahead of any other. Cornelius told him that court was perhaps the best place a good citizen could be "made" and the recipe always includes humility. Cornelius also taught him that if no humility could be found, the disposal of his life was the best way to preserve peace and keep tax revenues flowing. Caleb passively disagreed. He thought something between these two extremes was possible, but it would require some education tactics that his uncle didn't use.

The report stated that he was arrested three days ago after stealing bread from a shop owner near the arena. It also said he attempted to escape as two of Caleb's soldiers pursued him. It also stated that he intentionally destroyed a set of butcher scales and two baskets of tomatoes on his path as he ran away from the authorities and the shop owner. If nothing else were true, it is evident that this man was attempting to avoid consequences long before he was arrested.

As the man defended himself with gestures and pleas for mercy, Caleb looked the man up and down. He appeared fit and capable of hard work. He could also tell that the man had made money in his lifetime and lost it, as his sandals were of the highest quality, as was the belt around his robe. Those two items are not made at the same shop, so Caleb knew he didn't steal them, at least not at the same time.

"He's guilty," Caleb said to himself. He knew it. For now, though, he desired to see the man's heart and see if he desired to become a good citizen.

Caleb watched the man's body language as he finished the tea and handed the empty cup back to the slave, keen to observe the man's response to the gift she gave him. He failed to make eye contact with the girl, nor did he offer any words of gratitude for her gift of hot tea. Caleb raised the cheek on the left side of his face and shook his head. He all but knew how this trial would end. Caleb jumped to another question that would give the man a final chance to humble himself. After all, if there is one thing that having a risen Messiah has taught him, it is that everyone deserves a second or perhaps a third chance. He remembers his cousin Eliza telling him something from the New Torah about forgiving seven times seventy-seven times, but that rule doesn't apply in Rome court.

"Take me to the moment that the shopkeeper and my soldiers claim that you took what was not yours," he said.

"What?" the man asked. Caleb changed the question, thinking that perhaps he didn't understand him.

"What made the act of taking bread but not paying for it the right thing to do?" Caleb asked. He hoped he would apologize and see that whatever he thought didn't justify taking from someone else.

"Centurion, I was hungry. I had not eaten the previous day and this baker had enough food for an entire village."

Caleb had observed his uncle respond to this sort of response many times. This hungry yet well-dressed man lacked impulse control. His lack of moral education was also on display, as he found nothing significantly wrong with taking a small amount of wealth from someone who could afford to lose a little of it.

"Where are you from?" he asked. Caleb knew to use the most basic Greek constructions with those who came here for work, as many barely knew the Empire's language.

"I come from Thessalonica," he said. Caleb had heard stories of this place when he was a boy growing up. Many of his father's friends would go there to serve the small but growing synagogues where the Messiah was proclaimed, but Caleb had not traveled there. He was tempted to begin speaking to the man in his native tongue, but he knew this could be problematic for the next 49 men awaiting trial. After all, few could believe that a Roman centurion could also be an archer from the tribe of Benjamin.

"My temptation is to allow you to make you pay restitution equal to four times what you stole, as it is written in Ebreet law. This is also acceptable in Roman law."

"Thank you, sir. I will gladly do it!" the man said, sensing he was about to be set free. Caleb was not so quick to end this man's trial.

"Cornelius would have cut off your hand," he said. He needed to let that statement sink in.

"I am grateful for your mercy," he said.

Caleb raised a finger and continued.

"However, I am greatly concerned about your lack of humility and gratitude."

He paused to make sure that everyone else awaiting trial was watching.

"Honorable centurion, I am grateful beyond words. You must believe me from every bone in my body!" he pleaded. Caleb raised his right hand and interrupted him. The soldiers guarding him knew that the right hand meant they would strike the man enough to mute him.

"Indeed, every bone in your body is speaking. Grateful, though, you are not."

The slave girl who had brought him the hot tea was now standing next to Caleb and she had taken a seat on the dais meant for Roman leadership. She called for the remaining servant to come to her and donned a pair of pure silver Bengals on each wrist. Each was worth as much as any of these men would earn in half a year. Caleb stood up and placed a robe of pure white around her, adorned with purple. Lastly, he put a silver ring on her finger and he looked the woman in the eye, grateful beyond words that she had agreed to come today.

The man on trial stood in horror, realizing what he had done. Caleb waited for Yael to take her seat. Then he stepped down from the dais, held his sword, and walked in front of the man. Caleb towered over him but he spoke calmly, knowing that 49 other trials would be governed by how this one ended. He was not about to waste his anger on a simple criminal.

"The woman who gave you the hot tea was a member of the house of Caesar and she is in the family of our emperor of the Roman Empire. The emblem on her ring proved it." Caleb took a brief pause to allow the evidence to seep into the minds and hearts of everyone watching. Then, almost as if it were effortless, he concluded the presentation side of the trial.

"She removed all her royal garbs to serve you tea so all could observe how grateful you are when you know nothing of those who are around you. Isn't this how you treated the shopkeeper?"

Caleb let his words linger in the arena as everyone watched Yael finish adjusting her clothing. No one spoke as the young servant Yael had kept with her now brought her their child. Caleb heard the little boy fussing and it made him smile. Everyone watched his wife in her grandeur as the wife of the Centurion of Caesarea prepared to nurse the next generation of great leaders. She was no longer a humble girl serving tea. She was the most powerful woman in any of the twelve tribes, and she had committed her life to helping him become a better man. His plan was working to perfection.

"To make matters much worse for you, this woman is my wife." Caleb put his arm on the man's shoulder and twisted his grip on his gladius so the blade was ready to be driven directly into the man's guts.

"And she is the mother to our beautiful baby boy who bears my father's name," he said.

With that, none of the men in shackles moved, and no sound came from their metal bindings.

"Therefore, I am increasing your punishment for your lack of gratitude. Good citizens are also grateful citizens. In addition to paying back four times what you stole, I sentence you to one year working in the city latrines. You will sleep with the lepers and appear before me at the end of that year. Tell me what you have learned. Don't be alarmed, however. Some of the men in line may be joining you." He looked up at the other men and all of them were pale and speechless. While he maintained eye contact with the next one in line, he rapidly sheathed his blade, turned, and walked back toward his wife.

"Thank you. See you tonight," he quietly told her.

"Caleb, I am proud of you. Uncle Cornelius, your mother, and your father would be proud of the man you are becoming," Yael said, staring into his eyes. Her nurturing words melted the young man's heart. Once Yael was gone, Caleb returned to the trials that awaited him.

"Next?" he yelled as he signed the report and handed it back to the scribes to record his verdict.

# Chapter 2:
# Discipline, Crucifixion, and the Fruits of the Spirit

With his first day in court complete, Caleb went to his office at the harbor. Two lieutenants were waiting for him and they gave him their report on the insurrectionist named Menes. Tomorrow was Shabbat for the local people and a day of rest for all those working on the empire's construction projects. In a few hours, it would be mid-afternoon on the last day of the week when all the laborers typically gathered to collect their weekly wages before what usually became a night of debauchery and whoring by the port. Caleb needed to decide this man's fate

and he had a hunch that he wouldn't like the route his men would suggest to him.

Caleb knew Menes' story. Menes publicly ridiculed the work foreman, telling him Egyptian architects would not allow such low-quality water transport systems to be built. In addition to telling them to start over and build the system the Egyptian way, Menes cursed their efforts to finish the project ahead of schedule and under budget. He knocked over scaffolding, requiring that the laborers rebuild it, and he would urinate in the paint, diluting it. When reprimanded and told to get back to work, he would spit on the foreman and continue swearing until he was struck by one of the soldiers. Yet, these beatings did not seem to deter Menes. Now, Caleb had to get involved.

Caleb had already spoken to and publicly struck the Egyptian warrior after his first act of insurrection, and Menes showed no remorse for his actions or words. Caleb knew the Egyptian language from his time in Crete with Cornelius. He told him to shut up or risk death the Roman way. Caleb knew Menes understood him by the way he looked at him and the change in his breathing. Menes was not expecting an Ebreet man and Roman leader to know his language and perhaps Caleb was counting on that discrepant event to invoke change. Alas, it did not.

"Centurion, he continues to make trouble. He is giving opinions on matters that don't concern him, and he spit on another guard while everyone was watching."

"Damn it!" Caleb said. Caleb shook his head in disgust as the lieutenants reminded him that Menes was part of a group of hooligans that had attacked and killed Roman soldiers in the port of Heraklion on the island of Crete. The men in charge of the Cretan docks were friends of Cornelius and Valentina and they allowed Menes and the surviving remnant to live as an act of mercy. However, because of his actions, he was enslaved. It now looked like that mercy act in Crete was a wasteful one. After all, not everyone does the right thing when they are given a second chance.

Caleb knew it was against Roman law to punish a man who had not first been warned. He made it a point to tell his lieutenants of the words he had already shared.

"I told Menes to do as he was told, pay taxes on his wages, and respect those in authority over him. If he had listened to me, he would be freed after two years."

Caleb paused and nodded his head. He would be a hypocrite if he didn't honor his word, which he promised Uncle Cornelius he would not do. He repeated what he had already told Menes.

"I also told him that if he did not comply, he would die a horrific death in front of the men he was attempting to entertain."

Caleb's men looked at each other.

"Is it that time, then?" they asked.

"I am afraid so. Bring the man at the set time and make the preparations we have practiced," Caleb said in the calmest voice possible.

As the men turned and left him, Caleb shook his head, swearing under his breath. Today was Caleb's first day to oversee payday without his Uncle Cornelius to consult with. He had seen his uncle do what he was about to do and he all but promised himself that he would do everything possible not to. Yet here he was, breaking a promise he made to himself and Eliza when he was a teenager when he killed a Roman soldier defending his parents. He was about to kill a man in front of others to make a point.

Cornelius had lived the life of a Centurion for more than 40 years. He told Caleb that these moments were unavoidable; Caleb knew this task must be done. When his mind returned after, he found that his lieutenants had left him and he was alone. He left the office and walked to find a place where he could be in private and out of earshot. He began to pray with words his uncle used in a similar situation, all the while shaking his head in disbelief that he could come up with no better solution than his uncle did. He dared not let his men know of his spiritual dilemma, so he spoke in a guttural form of Aramaic that few could understand unless they were Ebreet themselves.

"My Lord, I am a warrior who serves both men and You. I discipline men and you discipline me. This man's choices require I kill him the way that your son died, and I do not like that I am instigating this bitter cup." He ground his teeth and exhaled with authority after he found himself holding his breath.

"Please have mercy on me for what I am about to do. Please do not let it impact my family or the men who serve under me. Please help me maintain control of my emotions." He repeated these verses in every language he knew, parsing his words to find additional meaning that might grant him peace.

"I already hate this job!" he said, starting to argue with God. He had his decision to speak the way he did to Menus and he hated that he needed to keep his promise to Cornelius. His men would lose respect for him if he didn't keep his word in front of them as well. There was no way to escape what must be done.

His grip on his gladius had turned his knuckles white and all the veins in his arm were pulsing. He looked down and realized that he didn't remember unsheathing it. He ever-so-slightly shook his head back and forth and he quietly let what seemed to be a river of tears flow from his eyes. As his prayers came to an end, he sheathed his blade, raised his hands to head, and said, "Take this bitter cup from me. Amen."

He turned and walked back towards where his men were gathered, attempting to act as if nothing happened. His uncle had made it a point to tell him that his façade of readiness would be a permanent part of his life as he blended his belief in Yeshua with his life as a centurion, and he must make peace with its necessity. Alas, his uncle did not learn how to do that, and Caleb had no idea how to either.

As the afternoon approached, Caleb found the Roman accountants in their tent and told them to bring 10% extra coin. He also told them to send a messenger to tell him when they were coming to distribute weekly pay. Caleb also checked in with the five men on today's crucifixion team to ensure they would have the holes dug and the wood ready before Menes was brought forward. He told the accountants to set up their tables directly in front of the site of the crucifix, requiring that all men see Menes on the cross as they receive their weekly pay. As the time to begin approached, Caleb told his lieutenants to bring Menus to him when prompted.

Moments later, Caleb sent a message to all the foremen to bring the men to the fields where they temporarily tented. Once the men heard that it was time to go to the tents, they knew that work was over for the week and it was time to party. Caleb stood at the front of the group of nearly a thousand men, sitting on a tall horse. He raised a single hand to let them know to be quiet. Once all the men had stopped talking, he began to speak. He used Greek, but he would occasionally repeat himself using Egyptian and Farsi, as many enslaved Egyptians and Assyrians like Menes were in the crowd.

"Men, today is payday. The foremen tell me that we are ahead of schedule and on budget. This is good news to Caesar and it can be accredited to the good work that you are doing. Well done!"

He paused for a moment to let the men clap and express some joy. Once they had their moment, he raised his hand again.

"However, there is an injustice that we must address. We are required to display fair and efficient administration of justice, as most of you have no experience with consistent and honorable authority."

Many men had seen others commit violent crimes without being punished in their home cultures. Caleb would not let that pattern exist while he was in charge of Caesarea and this next moment was his chance to change the hearts of these men.

He turned to his lieutenants and spoke loudly.

"Bring forward the insurrectionist Menes."

Menes was quickly brought in front of Caleb, with his hands tied behind his back and his feet in tight shackles and heavy chains. He had a muzzle over his mouth, so he could not cry out and curse as he tended to do. Caleb stepped down from his horse and approached Menus. The soldiers cleared a semi-circle so all the men could come forward and see what was about to happen. This, too, was something that they had practiced.

"Menes, I warned you and beat you only two weeks ago to cease your behavior. You failed to heed my warning and instead acted insolent and cursed at your foreman. Rome has no room for those who choose not to learn or comply with our requirements. You have been given chances to change, but you didn't. As such, you must die."

Caleb knew that he must control his emotions and not allow his tone to waver as he pronounced judgment. He mounted his horse while Menes attempted to yell through his muzzle. Nothing came out other than squelched tones without meaning. Caleb paused, nonetheless, to make sure everyone could see that the Egyptian was resisting his judgment and that resistance was futile. He repeated himself in many languages to make sure everyone in the crowd understood him. However, for the rest of the trial, he spoke Greek.

"Your choices in life are now greatly reduced. In a moment, I will have your muzzle removed and I expect you to answer this question for me. Will you allow my men to punish you without resistance, or will you continue to fight us? If you are courageous and choose to comply, I will send three months' wages to your family in Alexandria and tell them you died honorably. If you resist, you will still die, and no word or money will be sent home."

Caleb gestured to his men to remove the man's muzzle. Once he did, Menes began to scream in Egyptian. Caleb knew what he was saying but most present did not.

"You are bastards. You take our land and make us work the land you think you own! You, Palestina, think all this land is yours. It belongs to Egypt! You are scum. You are thieves!" he said. With those words, Caleb gestured to the men to put the muzzle back on the man.

"Very well. You shall die and none other than those here now shall know."

Caleb gestured to the five men to begin their work and he moved his horse to the edge of the circle so all the men could watch. His crucifixion team had practiced this procedure and their handiwork was now the center of everyone's attention. Several of Caleb's soldiers unsheathed their gladius as a statement not to intervene with the punishment.

The men placed a large, wooden cross made of cedar on the ground, and they placed Menes' body on it. The two largest men put their knees on his leg and ankle chains, one on each side of the cross, and they held the man's legs stationary. The blacksmith in the crew had the most critical job as it was uniquely his responsibility to drive in the three spikes as quickly as possible. The men used the design of the shackles and the weight of the chain to forcefully cross his legs and hold them steady for the blacksmith. Once the top leg was directly above the heart of the wood on the cross, the blacksmith would strike the hammer into the bones above the ankle using his longest and sharpest spike. The first strike needed to break the bone in the top leg and come out the back side of the leg. He would then reposition the lower leg to make sure it was directly above the upper leg. Once they were set, he struck one time again. If the two strikes were successful, the spike would go the way through the top and bottom leg. Hopefully, a small portion of the spike would also enter the cross. Finally, the third and final strike would drive the spike into the heart of the cross such that he could no longer move his legs. This group had practiced this procedure at least 20 times using dead laborers and they were familiar with the effort and time needed. As

Caleb predicted, the legs were secured to the cross before all those watching had breathed ten times.

Once the legs were nailed to the cross, his group knew that Menes would enter a state of shock and his resistance would fade. The blacksmith was quicker with the arms and each of the remaining spikes required two strikes before Menes was completely attached to the cross. The blacksmith pulled hard on the top of each spike to make sure they were securely in the wood and then nodded to the others. The blacksmith removed the muzzle on the man and poured a bucket of water on his head, momentarily snapping him out of shock. As the blacksmith stepped away from the man, the other four men in the crucifixion crew lifted the cross with ropes until the base dropped into the hole. As soon as it went into the hole, the team stepped away and allowed the man to be the focus of all eyes.

With the shock temporarily removed, the screams of death created captivating sounds that are outside of the realms of describable. Several men vomited as they watched Menes express fear and disbelief that all that remained was excruciating breaths as he tried to shift his weight back and forth from his legs to his arms until he could do it no more. Then asphyxiation would begin and the horror that came from his mouth would shift to horror on his face as his last moments would be wrought with unsustainable efforts to breathe, speak, and inevitably seek forgiveness.

Caleb knew that all in attendance would be horrified by what they were about to hear and see; at that moment, the Centurion of Caesarea's words would have their most significant impact. He guided the horse near the crucifix, faced the men, and spoke, making eye contact with as many of them as he could.

"Each of you will receive 10% extra coin today. It is your reward for working hard and getting done ahead of schedule." Many men stopped looking at the dying man and his agony as they heard they were about to receive extra pay. Greed remained one of the few emotions greater than horror. The men nearest Menes remained too stunned to speak or applaud the additional wages, but those in the middle and back applauded the bonus.

"Men, you have tomorrow off. Do not do anything that will make you end up like Menes of Alexandria. Today, he died a preventable death. Do as you are told and you will make coin to provide for your family. Fight the ways of Rome, and you will die as he just did. The choice is yours," he said.

As Menes faded, his attempts to cry out for mercy and forgiveness became quieter and less impactful. For his part, Caleb acted as if he could hear nothing. He had spoken loud enough so that he drowned out any sounds from Menes.

Caleb turned his horse away from the crowd and walked towards the sea, allowing the horror of crucifixion to perform its magic as the center of everyone's attention. As Caleb departed, the accountants brought forth two chests of copper, bronze, and gold coins and set up their table in front of the cross. As soon as they sat down, the men began queuing in front of them to collect their wages. Most would take their pay, go to the docks, and get drunk at a tavern. However, no one in line talked as they received their pay. Menes' death was doing its job, or at least Caleb hoped.

"Name?" the accountants asked as each man stepped to the front of the line. After the men spoke their names, the accountant recorded that they had been given their wage for that week and received a handful of coins of various types they could use throughout the port. All the while, the men stared at Menes in disbelief at what was happening. A few men would pray for him, and perhaps another ten men vomited as they passed below him after receiving their pay and were required to walk underneath the cross.

The process repeated itself until the last man had received his weekly pay. All the while, Menes' spirit faded from his body. Once the last man had been paid, Caleb's team drove a spear into his side, ending his suffering. Once the last of his lifeblood had poured from where the spear entered his side, the men took him from the cross and disposed of his body.

Caleb watched from horseback as the body got carried off. He honestly didn't know what his men were about to do with it. He didn't care either. He slowly rode his horse back to the middle of the field and one of the accountants approached him, gave him his weekly pay, and wished him a good holiday. Once the accountants and soldiers left, he was alone in a field where nearly a thousand had been moments earlier. The cross was gone as well, but the Menes' blood was all over the Judaean soil as a reminder of his life and death.

Caleb took a deep draft of water from the skin his wife had filled for him that morning. He shook his head, wishing it was wine. The day was ending and he felt the temperatures were already dropping. He closed his eyes and took a deep breath of the cool air, pausing to reflect. He could not believe that he had just killed a man to ensure the peace of others.

He remembered the first time he watched Cornelius crucify a man for noncompliance with the mandates of the empire, forcing the offender to die a slow death in front of the others. In his lament, he remembered his uncle's words.

"Young man, life is not fair, and no man can know everything before administering justice. Publicly sacrificing this man's life will save others, whether you like to hear it or not. Remember, our God has always required a blood sacrifice for sin. First, it was the temple. Then, it was Yeshua himself. Rome is no different. You got to trust me on this."

Cornelius' teaching spoke to him that day in a factual way, with no effort to appeal to his heart. There was no heart when it came to orchestrating a man's death and reconciling it. The words he used were logical, but he felt near powerlessness as he pondered how he could make sense of death by crucifixion as a form of preventative justice. Caleb didn't know what he was feeling, but he didn't like that it was basting in anger and betrayal.

The anger was now boiling through the powerlessness. Caleb had been taught that Yeshua grants a peace that the world cannot understand. He had no such peace.

"Where in the hell is the peace you promised?" Caleb screamed out. No one was there to hear it. Once again, he looked down and found that his sword was in his hands.

His wife and cousin knew that he would yell out during his sleep. Caleb thought no one had heard his tirades, but these women had lost count of the number of times he had done it. They loved him, nonetheless. Indeed, the two of them would often hold hands and listen to his rage. Eliza had read during her studies that King David did the same thing, and she often would tell her sister that by watching Caleb, she could gain a better understanding of the words of the Psalmists. Yael would look at her when she said that, then force herself to smile yet cry.

At this moment, Caleb detested himself, Rome, and his choice to take the job of centurion. The weariness of sending a man to a horrific public death was against his being. All he wanted to do was ride this horse home, drink wine, and lay with his wife until these feelings disappeared. Then more wisdom from his uncle came to mind.

"I know how much you love our wife. I say this to you. If you love her, do not talk to her about what happens when you administer this sort of justice. Your pain will not be mitigated by revealing the horror of a crucifixion that you have ordered, and her heart will become another preventable casualty. Come and talk to me instead. A man's mortality is not the job of the woman to navigate, just as childbearing is not the man's job to understand."

Caleb nodded as if Cornelius was standing next to him and he spit on the ground in disgust at what he had just done. He paused a moment to identify his emotions; his wife taught him to do that. Loneliness was undoubtedly the strongest emotion, closely followed by self-loathing.

After Caleb returned his horse to the Legion's stable, he began walking home.

"My Lord, leadership is lonely," he prayed out loud. Now, instead of screaming to the Lord as he walked, he talked to Him as a friend the rest of the way home, just as his mother used to when she wrestled with a social wrong.

"I do not like this curse. I do not like to be the one who judges and administers justice. I am scared that you will judge me," he said.

He was almost home and nearing the stairs leading up to his family's compound on the top of the hill. The loneliness was accumulating, and the stairs would be solemn. Perhaps he would purchase some flowers at the bottom of the hill and give them to his wife. Maybe he would buy sweets for his uncle, aunt, and servants.

Perhaps he would drink two flasks of wine instead. It didn't matter as long as he didn't have to keep his current state of mind for much longer.

Yet his thoughts returned to what would happen when he stepped back into his family's compound and discarded the title of the centurion of Caesarea. He would be a father, husband, nephew, and occasional dishwasher.

He loved those healthy roles. He loved washing dishes when Yael gave the servants the day off. While he wore his old tunic and cleaned the clay plates that the family ate off of, he was nothing, but another member of a loving family doing his share of the chores. Cleaning the house would remove the self-loathing that sometimes haunted him as soon as he made it through the gates and took off his military gear for the weekend. He knew that he couldn't bring home stories of the horrors that he participated in. Cornelius was right; his wife and son deserved better.

He paused to remind himself how his fate brought him to this place. His life was ridden with injustice and he had no idea why he couldn't just live with himself. After all, Roman soldiers murdered his father and mother for their faith when he was a teenager. His wife was raped by Caesar's family when she was 16, and he swore he would kill the man who did it if their paths crossed. His cousin Eliza watched her parents taken off to slavery and they all watched as their school was burned by soldiers who were intent on destroying the teachers and the places where they learned about the Messiah. Now he was the most powerful man within two days' horseback ride in any direction, yet he felt that he was just as enslaved to Roman law as his aunt and uncle were. He felt as diminished as the slaves building the great pyramids. He and Menes probably had a lot in common in their hearts.

Yet he knew a living Yahweh and memories of all that he had done for him made him smile.

"Thank you, my Lord," he said, knowing that the people in his house at the top of the stairs loved him. His uncle was far more than an adopted family member now. He was his mentor and guide. He decided not to buy anything special for the weekend but instead gave

10% of his pay to a beggar at the bottom of the stairs. He had plenty of wealth and Eliza had taught him that nothing helps you break out of your mindset like giving to others. The beggar thanked him repeatedly, giving Caleb his first smile in a long time.

The smile remained as he neared the top of the steps. He needed to talk to his uncle. Cornelius has killed more people than anyone he has personally known. He wondered how it was possible that a man who killed so much could be capable of so much love. His uncle knew Simon Peter, and Simon Peter knew Yeshua. Cornelius led Shabbat services and had baptized hundreds into the faith in the spring in his family's compound.

He hoped Yael wouldn't ask him about his day. He quickly prayed she wouldn't detect that he was lying to her when he answered her. Instead, he changes his thoughts.

"Lord, protect my wife from her curious thoughts. Protect her from the words I will speak while I sleep this night. Protect her from any evil I may bring into our home."

He reached a section of the steps where his servant on sentry duty could see that he was nearing home and dinner would be awaiting him as soon as he entered the house. He had one last prayer.

"Please don't let my cousin Eliza come for a visit today or tomorrow. She can see through me too easily."

And with that, he reached the iron gate. He knew the sweat and exhaustion of the run would disguise the damage done to his soul. All he heard were his own words repeated in his head as he stood before the men, pointing at Menes as he was crucified, telling them how they would all end up like him if they failed to comply.

"My Lord, please put a spirit of submission on this city's laborers and their hearts so I don't have to kill another man."

He stepped into the compound, hoping to find his uncle before he found his wife. The old man stood near the gate as he entered. No one else was there, almost as if he expected him. Caleb's sanity boiled over and he knew he could not speak without an outpouring of emotion.

Cornelius held open his arms as Caleb ran to him like an 8-year-old boy might run to his father after he came home from an unsuccessful hunt. The two men were taller than anyone else, with powerful frames and beards on their faces.

"Payday?" asked Cornelius as he held Caleb's cheek and looked him in the eye.

And with that question, the walls came down. Caleb began sobbing uncontrollably, unable to finish any sentence he had started. He fell to his knees, allowing Cornelius to place a hand on his shoulder as he exalted him in a prayer of intercession. The pain reminded Caleb of the afternoon he had to put down his dog. Cornelius lifted him back up and put his massive hands on Caleb's face.

"I already told the women folks that we would be back later. For now, let's go, boy," said the wise master.

Cornelius held up the massive man as if he were a tree about to fall as they stepped back through the iron gate to take a seat on the bench outside their compound. Cornelius nodded to the servant on duty, signaling not to wait for them but to be with his family instead. The man bowed and quickly left.

Yael and Valentina had been watching everything from the kitchen door. As they stepped outside the gate and could no longer be seen, Yael blurted out, with a sense of panic to her mentor.

"Aunt Val, what can I do for him? He is my husband!" she pleaded as her tears began. Val smiled and cried as she watched Yael fall to pieces. She put her hand on her face and nodded, making no effort to hide her tears. She had been in Yael's sandals for nearly 50 years.

"He is my husband!" Yael repeated.

Val pulled Yael near her and she let the young woman pour out tears. Val smiled, held, and kissed the Yael on the cheek and the top of her head repeatedly as she sobbed uncontrollably.

"Little one, you are perceptive that he won't be OK today or tomorrow, but you must be patient. Just do as he asks, and don't ask him about what he just did. All you should know is that you have one task that can change everything," said Val.

"What! What is it?" said Yael, hungry for an answer to her pain.

"Pray." Val paused to let the power of the single word settle into her soul. Yael looked at her, wondering how such a simple thought and action could be, as she said.

"What? That is it? That is your only counsel?" Yael said, desperate for more information.

"Little One, pray for him without ceasing. Pray that he navigates what it means to be a man of God and a man of Caesar simultaneously." Val grabbed Yael's face and looked her in the eye.

"This pain you so clearly see is part of his job. These moments will always be a part of him. It is our job not to let them define him." Val hugged the woman again and rocked her back and forth, allowing Yael to let go of all her tears. She kept a firm hold on her, keeping her head on her shoulder. She whispered to her that this would pass and he would come back and love you.

Val dared not tell the truth. She dared not let Yael see the depth of her pain, too. She wondered if there might be a day when she could tell the young woman that she had spent decades of her life watching her husband climb those same stairs on payday, soaking in guilt, shame, and pain. She had seen her husband wash off blood that he couldn't talk about. She had seen him sit in front of their outdoor firepit, where they would celebrate Shabbat, and he would cry from the bottom of his heart. She had watched him pick up rocks and throw them as hard as he could, swearing and fighting with God. And she had seen him lay in the fetal position, unable to move. Then, he would arise, tuck in his shirt, and come inside. Valentina would look at her husband and mourn that she couldn't understand what it meant to be a centurion working for Nero.

For now, Val needed to be courageous for Yael. If Caleb was going to be a better man, Yael needed to be a better woman. No matter the cost.

For a moment, Val considered telling Yael the truth. Perhaps it could help to let her know that Cornelius had nightmares from events decades earlier. She remembered the last time they were in Rome. He had an outburst defending an event that he had allowed years earlier, and he nearly drew his blade on a Roman senator. It would not help Yael to hear that her husband might not heal, but she could provide her with hope.

"Come, let's sit and wait for them to return. If I know Corn, they won't be long. He knows what he is doing," she said.

The truth was that Cornelius didn't know what he was doing. All her husband could do was sit with Caleb as the young man vented of the evils in the world to his mentor. All Cornelius could offer was the importance of surviving a moment using the power of a great savior and the teachings of a short and fat Simon Peter, prone to drinking too much wine, and who spent a few days in their family compound a long time ago.

# Chapter 3:
# Death Bed

"Woman, bring me another blanket!" said the old centurion with an authority in his voice that had been fading all week. His wife and most of his family were already gathered around him, as it was obvious that his days were near their natural end. Wintertime in the land of Manasseh is cold but there was solace because the Mediterranean Sea was visible in the distance outside of the walls of their hilltop home. Whitecaps rolled across the distant sea as ships entered and left the harbor, carrying their wares around the Roman Empire. Every sailing nation's language could be heard on the docks and Caesarea was a melting pot of trade, second only to Rome. All of that grew under Cornelius' faithful guidance.

Two days ago, his servants had taken the family's largest table and converted it into a makeshift bed so their master could spend as much time outside as he could now that his days were counted. Cornelius insisted on spending all day outside, no matter what his wife said. He wanted to end his days on his terms, in a place of his choosing. He had spent most of his life outside, and he was going to die outside.

"Corn, it is cold out here! Let us take you inside, OK?" Val would ask. She knew he wanted to make every one of his remaining days matter, but it was a cold Januarius day and no one wanted to watch him die in the cold. Everyone knew the old man would not live until the weather warmed at the end of Martius. For now, his wife was buying time until the last of his family could make the trip to Caesarea for his death. Yael had already sent out letters to all his family and she expected the last of his relatives to come later today.

She had no idea how much Cornelius could process all the chatter around him, but as long as he was breathing, he could bark orders to his wife. Yael was barely 22 years old but she knew he fed on laughter and sounds from people that weren't words. Most of the time, his eyes were closed; however, he would smile when he heard someone laugh, especially Yael's two-year-old son Mishi.

A sound at the iron gate got everyone's attention. Soon, the courtyard was filled with sounds of Ebreet and Gentiles greeting one another, and another smile took form on Cornelius' face. Cornelius knew that voice and he had asked about her nearly every day since he moved outside. Val took that moment to talk to him.

"Look, my love. Guess who is here?" said Valentina as four people approached his outdoor living arrangement. A young woman ran to him the fastest. As soon as she arrived, she took his hand, looked him in the eye, and began to cry. He began to laugh but it was interrupted by strong coughing that came from deep within his chest.

"Uncle, it's me, Eliza," she said, bending over to kiss him. Once she did, Eliza looked up and made eye contact with her sister, and they began crying together. Yael wiped the tears from Eliza's eyes and stepped backward to give her sister time with the dying warrior. Eliza surveyed his body and could see how he had diminished, and she returned her focus to his face to avoid the pain of looking at his frailty.

"I am so glad we made it," said Eliza. Yael whispered something to her sister but Cornelius couldn't hear it. All he knew was that they were laughing and that made him smile. However, Cornelius' cough came back and he began a hoarse exchange of air. Once he stopped talking, he spoke to Eliza.

"Oh, finally, you are here! The one with the mouth!" he said, causing everyone to laugh. As the laughter died down, Yael began small talk with her sister. Their mother was next to them, but she didn't speak, letting the girls catch up with each other first. Eliza told Yael that she hadn't found anyone who shared her lifestyle that she would be interested in marrying, which was all Yael wanted to hear about. Her mother was equally interested, but she learned everything she needed by listening to the two of them talk. It had been that way since they were teenagers and they had adopted Yael.

Yael and her husband Caleb had lived with Corn and Val for over three years. Cornelius had mentored Caleb throughout that time, and Caleb had recently taken over the last of the centurion's responsibilities for the port city of Caesarea. Meanwhile, Val had been mentoring Yael, which was perhaps a harder task. The centurion's wife bore at least as much hardship as the warrior, but she stayed at home most days, stuck in her thoughts. Caleb, at least, got out every day. With a toddler and another one on the way, Yael had limited opportunities to meet new people.

Everyone in the community knew that Yael and Caleb were orphans. Eliza was their common connection and a great stabilizing force. She was Caleb's cousin and lifetime playmate. It was during the time the three of them spent together that Caleb asked Yael to marry him. Eliza had watched every moment of their courting and engagement, and she couldn't have been happier for them. The three of them were a unique team and adored spending time together.

Caleb and Eliza grew up together, and Yael joined them much later. Yael made a near-instantaneous upwardly social motion when she stood with Caleb and broke the glass to become his wife. In three months, she went from being a slave within the walls of the royal palace to becoming the wife of a centurion, one of the Roman military's power positions. She was also the spouse of one of the most powerful men in all of Judah, with nearly one out of ten people of Ebreet descent living within a day of Caesarea, the port that he governed. Her humble upbringing had to be set aside; she found herself handling affairs of the estate of one of the greatest men in her people's history. Now, they also had a little boy and they were living the challenges of marriage and children. Yael went from slave to wife, mother, head of state, and keeper of an estate with seven servants and their families.

Yael's adoptive mother, Katya, was Yael's most frequent visitor throughout. Occasionally, Eliza could join them, and the three women would have a grand time. However, they all lived in different places and it was more difficult for them to come together. This compound on the top of the hill outside Caesarea was, by far, the best place to gather. It had ample housing and was safe for the children to play. The servants were fully integrated into their lives, and Ebreet and Gentiles came and went freely. The facility was protected and beautiful, just like all the women under Caleb and Cornelius' care.

This time, the gathering would not be one of joy. It was obvious that Cornelius' pending death would be the focus of this visit, but the girls would share all they could while they were together.

"Where is father?" Yael asked.

"He will be here tomorrow. There were new settlers in Correae and your father needed to take care of a few items before leaving. He will be here soon!" said Kayta. Matthew was a man of influence in their village and he could not leave as quickly as the others when news came of Cornelius' pending passing.

Their family dynamic was unique. Yael and Caleb had a son named Mishi. Her mother had a son named Aaron, nearly the same age as Yael's son, in addition to her two grown daughters. Katya was used to receiving all the jokes when people would ask her if the person in front of them was her child or grandchild, as both of them were the same age. Yet their situation worked. Katya spent nearly every other month with her daughter and grandson in Caesarea; they all had their own room. Katya's husband, Matthew, was OK with the arrangement. He was senior enough in the community that he joined her at least half the time. Meanwhile, Eliza accepted the calling of Rabbi Dor and trained to become a Rabbi in the tradition of Melchizedek. She lived and worked in Gaza, training to carry the message of a Risen Messiah that her aunt introduced her to. Eliza was much less frequent of a guest, but she also had the best stories of what she had been doing. Eliza had learned the art of healing and counseling under Rabbi Dor and her sensitivity to the Holy Spirit continued to grow.

Eliza had multiple spiritual gifts; she could speak in tongues and she could call upon the Holy Spirit to heal in times of need. She was voluptuous and stunningly beautiful with dark Ebreet Features. When she walks with Caleb, they appear as if they are the King and Queen of Judah, though none of them exist anymore. Caleb and

Eliza had been very affectionate throughout their childhood and neither of them hesitated to kiss the other and tell each other that they loved the other. However, Caleb would also carry Eliza around and tickle her like she was a teenager and she would hit him and scream, telling him to stop.

The arrival of this group revived the better side of what was left of Cornelius. Katya set her grandson on his lap, as Cornelius loved little ones.

"Katie, what do we have here?" he asked. Katie was the nickname her family used for her. Katya pulled Cornelius' remaining hair off to the side so that he could be respectable. Cornelius touched the little boy and identified him.

"Little Aaron, you are getting so big!" Cornelius said once she put the little boy in his lap.

"Your grandfather missed you," Katya said. Cornelius babbled and played with the young boy, tickling him much like how Caleb would tickle Eliza. This allowed Yael and Eliza some more time to talk without interruptions. Eliza jumped right in with her stories.

"I am learning a lot from Dor. Dor says that he will be sending me out on my own very soon, and it scares me," she said.

With that, she told a long story about how a boatful of burn victims and refugees ended up in Gaza, and she went down to pray for them. Nearly all of them had burns on their skins, but Eliza and another one of Dor's disciples healed them, and there were no signs or scars three days later. Eliza was so dry in the storytelling that her nonjudgmental sister told her she needed to spice her storytelling up a bit. As her stories of miracles neared an end, she switched to topics about things she couldn't discuss with her rabbi.

"Dor said that the most important skill I needed to learn was counseling if I was to serve our community under Roman occupation." She paused and looked at the entrance to the kitchen. She knew that Yael could be trusted with the most intimate thoughts, and she needed to tell her what was on her mind.

"Yael, I don't know if this is what I really want to do. I love working with groups and seeing them all interact, but working one at a time with refugees is not my specialty," she said. Yael laughed.

"I totally disagree. I was there when you talked to Emperor Titus. I watched him melt like butter. Eliza, you are excellent one-on-one," Yael said. Eliza realized what she said, and they joked for a moment before Yael got around to answering her sister.

"Eliza, I am a mother and a wife now. I don't understand the world of a rabbi that you live in. I am not a healer. I am not a teacher. I am not gifted in tongues. However, I know you and have seen some of your best and worst moments. You love to travel, meet new people, and see things. You are also a fantastic teacher. I think you are in the right place with Dor." Her mother had quietly returned as Aaron had fallen asleep. She didn't hesitate to join in her daughters' conversation. There was hot tea on the stove and Katie poured each of her daughters a cup. The girls were talking about marriage and they asked her a question. Both girls honored their mother's input.

"I don't see you settling down anytime soon, Eliza. Dor isn't the one who called you. The world is calling you," Katie said. Eliza smiled and looked down to the ground again before looking back at the two greatest women in her life. All the women agreed with Katie.

"One day, I want to have what you two have," Eliza said, pointing at Aaron and Mishi.

"Little One, wait upon the Lord. It will come. Remember Elizabeth? She was older than Val when she had John," Katie told her daughter.

"But I don't want to wait that long!" she said, making everyone, including Val, laugh hard. Yael needed to catch the others up on what was happening with Caleb.

"Sometimes, Caleb comes home, kisses me, and takes little Mishi away for a walkabout. He is gone a long time and the baby is always asleep when he comes back in. I can see that Caleb has been crying. He holds me tight at night but often has nightmares and wakes up screaming. He apologizes and goes back to sleep, but I can tell that the centurion's job is a great burden that affects him when he sleeps. He is a good man, but his heart seems always to be wounded."

"Are you asking me to heal him? You know I can't heal that, right?" Eliza said. She could see that Yael was crying and felt great empathy for her husband's pain.

Eliza reached out and stroked Yael's beautiful black hair, exquisitely combed and scented with perfume. Yael wore perfectly clean clothing and put on fresh cotton garments each morning. The wife of the centurion from Caesarea was truly a kept woman, but she remained an orphan at heart, trying to heal and help a man who came home wounded most nights. Her physical wealth was beyond measure, but her emotional wealth was on its last reserves.

"I can't heal him, but I can counsel you. You have certainly done it for me," Eliza said, hugging her sister. Eliza knew it was time to use all her counselor training and care for her sister. Over the course of two cups of tea, Eliza listened, asked questions, and smiled when Yael smiled, allowing her sister a chance to feel safe as she told stories of Caleb's struggles. Soon, Eliza was wiping away her tears and drawing her sister into her chest as the depth and breadth of her fears were revealed. She feared Caleb would continue to erode and eventually take his own life.

"We will pray for him, but Yeshua needs to heal this in His own way," said Eliza with an authority that no other woman perhaps in all of Judah could say. Yael smiled but couldn't speak.

"Caleb is lucky to have you beside him through this," Eliza said.

"And I could not do this without Aunt Val. She is more precious to me than silver! I don't know what I will do after she and Uncle Corn are gone," said Yael.

"Let's go back outside and spend time with them while they are still here!" said Katie.

They found Cornelius in the middle of one of his fits of coughing. These spasms were commonplace for him. Whatever was in his lungs was getting worse and he was no longer responding to lemon and honey elixirs.

Once this current bout stopped, Val asked him an important question.

"Do you want your whiskey now?"

"I am dying, aren't I?" he rhetorically asked. Val looked at him and nodded, allowing some silent tears to fall. Val explained to the girls that during the last few months, Cornelius' solace was strong alcohol. He found that it would relieve him from the pain and the interruption caused by his coughing. He could drink two full cups of it and it quickly numbed his chest pain. However, it also made him drunk within a few minutes, and he had a brief period when his speech was intelligent and coherent.

"Everyone except Matthew is here now," said his wife. She knew that he didn't have time to wait until tomorrow, and he understood.

"Then, it is time. Bring the whiskey," he said. Katya went with her, returned with another blanket, and handed Yael's son back to her. Moments later, Val returned with a clear glass container filled with brown liquor.

Val knew it was Cornelius' final moment to invest in those he loved. She and he had talked, and he wanted to use it to address some unfinished business from Caleb and Yael's wedding three years earlier. She allowed him to have this as his last wish and she privately grieved for him, but she respected his choice. She told him she loved him and kissed him on the face as she handed him the whiskey.

After drinking the first cup of whiskey, Caleb helped him stand up from his makeshift outdoor bed and walk toward his favorite chair. Everyone moved out of the way as he gingerly took steps towards it on the edge of the flower garden. Once he arrived, he sat down without assistance and straightened his legs, contracting his muscles. His lower body remained solid and shapely, but everyone knew that his leg strength would soon follow his lung strength and nothing would be left. He held up his hands and reached out for someone to give him his grandchildren. Mishi and Aaron were placed on their grandfather's lap and he lifted his legs up and down to entertain the young boys.

"I want my girls next to me. Everyone else, step back!" he said with the authority that has always been his. His daughters Adi, Eliza, and Yael were all next to him within a moment.

"You girls know that my days are complete. Soon, I will have my questions answered when my Spirit meets Adonai. And I have a lot of them!" he said, raising a single finger to the sky. Everyone laughed. Despite his proximity to death, the older man's sense of humor remained.

"Yael, I want to talk to you first. I have one more lesson to teach you."

Yael bowed her head, not knowing what he was about to say. "Yes, uncle."

"You were given Eliza's ring when we had the funeral for Caleb's parents after your wedding. Can I see it again?" he asked. He coughed, but only lightly.

She quickly took it off and gave it to him. The day that Titus knew he was to die, he sent him one as well, but he never told anyone about it other than his wife. He wanted to see if his ring looked like hers. Once he saw that it did, he handed it back to her.

"I thought the citizenship that ring extended you would protect you, but Adonai has made me realize that you need more than membership in the emperor's house to be safe. That is why I am calling you next to me now. I have been working with your man a lot and he will need you more than I need Val. Whatever strength you believe that ring gives you, remember this. You will need to be stronger than that damn ring. Do you hear me?" he said.

"Yes, uncle," she said. She smiled and nodded, not sure of what he meant. He looked at Eliza and motioned for her to come to him.

"You, young Eliza, are known to challenge me publicly and not be struck down!" Everyone laughed as she reached out and held her uncle's hand. She removed his hair from his mouth and touched him on the head as he continued.

"If I remember, you said a girl should receive her father's blessing just as much as a boy, yes?" he asked, with a tone that demanded an answer.

"Yes, Your Grace!" she said playfully, making everyone laugh.

"I should have struck you for your insolence that day! You know that, right?" He paused for a moment and looked at the two boys in his lap before he continued. Eliza would never agree that the right thing to do was strike her for following what she felt the Lord was telling her to do.

"Instead, I was convicted by the Holy Spirit. That is why I call *you* girls next to me now."

He broke eye contact with her and spoke to Caleb and Valentina.

"Take these kids," he said. Caleb took his son and Valentina took Katie's son. Then he returned to his focus on the girls. He spoke first to his biological daughter.

"We gave you the name 'Adi' because we knew you would be the jewel of our lives. You did not disappoint. You are our daughter; whatever you wish to keep from all our possessions is yours. You get the first pick. I know your husband is a successful merchant who provides for you and keeps you happy, but you will always be my daughter. That is why I call you next to me first," he said. He took a few moments to breathe and refocus before continuing this effort. Everyone knew the effects of the alcohol would start soon, so no one interrupted his line of thought.

"I have been thinking and watching tradition change before my eyes. I was born to a powerful Roman military family in the heart of the glory that defines our Empire. I joined the military as my father and grandfather before me, and I had a successful career, thanks to your mother. When I was young, I was sent to this place. I learned the language and got promoted to the rank of Centurion when Caesarea was an undeveloped port. I did not love this place, but I loved my job and took pride in being the best at everything Rome asked of me."

"Then I met Peter and that changed everything. Before Peter, I only partially understood the Torah and Mishnah from our local synagogue. I knew Yahweh's heart and thought I knew how to follow him between soldiering and parenting. Heaven will tell how well I did."

He paused to take another drink of whiskey.

"There are many cultures in this city and I think Cornelius' culture needs to expand with it. My wife and I agree that we will start a new tradition today. I want you to share it with the other families you meet, whether they follow Yeshua or not."

He paused to take another sip of whiskey to snuff the burning pain in his lungs.

"In the same way that the hearts of a woman and a man grow when they have another child, I now think that the blessings a father bestows can grow in the same way. Yes, I already gave my blessing to

Caleb a few years ago, but Val and I have decided that a man can give another blessing or two." Everyone smiled.

"Yael, Adi, Katya, and Eliza, come and receive my blessing." Val knew this was about to happen, but no one else did. Since it was unheard of for a man to give his end-of-life blessing to a woman, everyone looked shocked. The seven servants immediately bowed to their knees, as it was their part to pray during these ceremonies.

Katya was the eldest, so she knelt and put her hand under Cornelius' thigh first. Once she did, her daughters followed, with one on each side of her. Adi took the other leg as her own, and all four women knelt and bowed their heads in reverence.

"Katya, you are the mother of these two and you carry the greatest burden. They are your legacy. Eliza and Yael, you must respect your mother and make her respectable in all the communities you visit." The two women looked up and nodded in agreement and submission to him. They could not share with words how important his discipleship was to them.

"Bow your heads," he said. He could not see that they already had.

For her part, Valentina stood behind her husband and adjusted his robes and blankets to make him seem dignified for perhaps the last time. Katya turned to each of her daughters, kissing them on the cheek and telling them that she loved them.

Valentina spoke up again with a bit of raw power in her voice.

"For Yahweh's sake, Caleb, put your hands on your wife's shoulders and stand with her! Your wife did that for you when you received your blessing, didn't she? What is wrong with you?" said Valentina.

"Yes, mum," he said as he stepped forward, humbly bowing his head and placing a hand on Yael's.

Cornelius needed to share a few more words before he could no longer.

"Hey," he said, getting the girls to look up.

"You girls know there is no precedent nor any mitzvah to follow. As such, I have made this with Val's help. This is the best a dying old man can do!" he said.

Cornelius raised his hands as he imagined Abraham and Isaac did, and he touched the heads of each of the girls.

"May you find the courage to help and serve others, no matter what they say or do.

"May you choose a path of integrity no matter what is perceived as correct.

"May you find peace during times of chaos and uncertainty that are part of being a wife and mother."

That last word stung Eliza in the heart. She was neither of those things, and it made her feel alone. She suddenly wondered if those words would be a dream she might not see come to pass. She was overcome by sadness and could no longer pay attention to the old man's last words.

"May you persevere through difficulties that will come your way."

"May your children make the world a better place for all, and may they spread the message of the Messiah, reborn and alive."

"And may you be fortified in the face of temptation." His speech was beginning to slur, and everyone knew he was starting to get drunk.

"And everyone said?"

Everyone quietly whispered, "Amen." Everyone knew what was next for Cornelius, the great centurion. Only time would dictate the moment when he breathed his last.

# Chapter 4:
# Funeral and Eulogy

It was the coldest day of the year thus far, and everyone at the old centurion's funeral wore layers of clothing to stay warm. The wind would come in spurts but when it arrived, it bit to the bones of those present. However, when it stopped, the air was crisp and clean, and the sun took a moment to remind everyone that warmth was always nearby.

From the perspective of the Roman military, the funeral would not fit the tradition. During a military funeral, a single coin was placed in the deceased mouth to pay for his safe passage to the underworld. Then his body was burned on a funeral pyre outside the city gate for all to see. It was a great honor to burn in front of everyone, as many would come and pay homage to the man and his life of service to the Empire. Ironically, the tales of his deeds and his impact on the Empire lasted as long as the fire burned, and it was essential to the family and his legacy to make the fire as big as possible.

Caleb had talked to the old man too many times when he was feeling grief and he knew that Cornelius wanted nothing that brought added attention to any death, especially his own. He had told Caleb that he had lost count of how many people he had killed and he didn't want anything to do with glorifying his death, no matter what his peers or members of the Senate said. Instead, he instructed Caleb to create a family gravesite on a remote corner of his property and then celebrate his life with family, friends, and servants. He and Caleb selected a burial location at the farthest corner of a field at the top of their estate. Caleb knew to trust his uncle and could see nothing wrong with defying much of the Senate to whom he now sent monthly reports. Instead, he merely informed the Senate in a letter that Cornelius would have a quiet family funeral.

Caleb had instructed the rabbi at their synagogue to have a private funeral, but the Rabbi could not control his tongue. The reality of overseeing the ceremony of a celebrity prospered more than Caleb's request to keep things quiet and the rabbi told everyone in the congregation about the event. In addition to the 600 men who reported to Cornelius, most of the city shop owners that Cornelius loyally visited made the trip up 300 stairs to say goodbye to their city leader. The local merchants closed their shops for the day to honor the man who kept their city safe from crime for nearly 40 years. The Senators from the region asked that the main road in town be renamed in his honor, but Caleb instructed the mayor to restore the original name. Eliza could not believe how many people came up the stairs, and she counted nearly 800 people present, not counting family members and servants.

Per Caleb's instruction, Cornelius' family and servants took turns digging the hole where his body would be placed near the top left portion of the plot. Since women were not allowed to participate in the digging, Yael decided to have the women help her fill a large water cistern with red wine. They had made drinking cups from sycamore tree leaves that all young girls learned to make with their mothers, and they placed as many as possible on a table next to the cistern. Everyone would get their serving with no concern for hygiene that comes from sharing cups.

Caleb and Yael had a life-shaping moment as the funeral started. Before his uncle died, he and Caleb laid out a few large stones to mark where Val would be buried and where Caleb, Yael, and his children would be laid to rest. Caleb had not yet told Yael that he wished to have four children with her, partly for fear of rejection and partly for a lack of thinking that he needed to do it soon.

Thinking nothing of his intentions, he placed four smaller stones on the ground next to the pair he set down for himself and his wife as their placeholders. The one on the far left had Caleb's first initial drawn on it with ash and next to his stone was one for Yael. It also had her first initial written in ash upon it. Young Mishi had his initials on his stone and the other three remained blank. There were spaces for their future spouses as well, as Caleb was thinking about legacy far into the future.

As people began to arrive, anxiety filled Caleb's heart, as his failure to communicate with his wife was about to be a public event. He had been so occupied with the funeral preparations and transition of all the jobs he was now responsible for that he had not prioritized talking to her about his family planning intentions. Cornelius had told him repeatedly to take his wife for a walk to this place and show her what he was thinking, but he never got around to it. When he saw her in the approaching crowd, his heart raced, and all his magical intentions were now free-floating in the wind as he knew he would have to watch his wife experience discovery without any discussion or opportunity for negotiation.

His situation got more complicated. Caleb made peace years ago that Yael and Eliza were more intelligent than he was, and he knew it would not be long before they sorted out what was happening. In addition, they held greater power with words than he did, and they knew how to dress down his being into that of a 14-year-old boy in a single breath. He was not ready to be ridiculed before his men and the leadership of the city he now ruled. He knew it wasn't their heart to hurt him, yet they knew how to do it in short order.

As the two women dearest to him in the world approached, he took his eyes off them and looked around at everyone else. All around him were the men who would now follow him. Some were three times his age, and many had been fighting for Caesar before he was born. All he could think of was whether his wife and sister would approve of his desire for three more children.

"Yeshua, please enter my wife's heart. Please soften her!" he pleaded in prayer as his wife took her place next to him. As she stood next to him at the hole in the ground, he reached out and held his wife's hand. Public displays of affection were non-existent in the Roman military. Still, Caleb could find no other way to share that he was on the edge of tears as he awaited his wife's response to her discovery of his intent. She looked up at him and began to look around, knowing he was giving her a clue.

As he expected, it took nearly no time for her to discover his intentions. Once she did, she looked up at him and stared into his eyes. She understood her husband's anxiety and she gently nodded her head in affirmation. Perhaps the man next to her was a great leader in Ebreet and Roman traditions, but at this moment, she held the hand of a scared and damaged boy who clung to his wife as his greatest strength. His soul was at her mercy and she looked up at him, just like Aunt Valentina would do.

She pointed a single finger at the stones representing Caleb's vision for her family. She turned her head to the side and smiled at her mom, quickly explaining what the stones meant. She returned her eyes to Caleb, this time letting a single tear of joy fall from her eye. She closed her eyes and nodded yes with authority. Her single nod made Caleb melt.

Caleb was wearing his most regal uniform and attire, including a ceremonial gladius, the hilt adorned with rubies and sapphires. He stood taller than anyone in attendance and the worth of his apparel was worth more than five years' wages. He knew he needed to look dignified for all to see as the inheritor of his uncle's legacy. He was literally the King of Caesarea and everyone knew it.

However, once Yael nodded yes, none of that mattered. He released his grip on his sword, and it slid back into its sheath. He bent over and kissed his wife. He whispered into her ear, using the moment to wipe a tear from his eye.

"OK?" he quietly asked, this time using words.

"Yes, of course. Caleb that is beautiful," she said. Caleb could not contain his joy and he whispered into her ear.

"Yael, I love you!" They embraced momentarily before she pushed him away and began speaking normally.

"Go! Our uncle's funeral demands your attention now. You are now the leader of all these men. They must be your priority," she said. Caleb agreed and reached down and drew forth his ceremonial sword. As he moved toward the head of the grave to stand next to the rabbi in charge, Eliza and Katya each blew him a kiss to show their approval of all that had just transpired. Eliza got his attention long enough to wink at him, causing him to smile. It was Eliza's approval, after all, that meant the most to him in this world.

His lieutenants brought forward Cornelius' body. He had been cleaned and now wore a new uniform. They placed him in the hole and Caleb rested the old man's sword on his chest. Cornelius had already given Caleb his battle helmet at his wedding to Yael. Caleb removed that helmet and placed it on Cornelius' chest, thereby returning it to its rightful owner. Caleb needed to demonstrate humility in front of his men if he expected them to do the same in the years to come. He quickly climbed out of the hole, stood at attention, and saluted his commanding officer for the last time. As soon as he did, all the men in Legion saluted the dead soldier. Cornelius' commanding officer took a knee of reverence as the old man captured everyone's attention for one final moment.

As Caleb expected, all the women left after the rabbi finished his words and the men took turns with the two shovels covering the body with dirt. The shopkeepers and soldiers began their march down the stairs after they each threw a shovel full of dirt on the dead man. All the while, Yael, Katya, and Eliza thanked them all for coming and offered them some wine from the cistern.

Once the mountaintop was clear of all but family and servants, Eliza and Adi took on a leadership role. They directed all the family and the servants to the entrance to the family estate in a walled enclosure that would take them out of the wind. Once they entered, they quickly walked toward two outdoor fires that had been lit and added more firewood to them. They provided much needed warmth after the ceremony. They huddled around the fires and sipped on wine while they waited for the men to finish the burial and return to the compound to get out of the wind.

Once the last of the dirt was on top of the burial mound, Caleb and two of Cornelius' most trusted servants placed the headstone that Cornelius had commissioned once he knew that the sickness in his lungs was not going to leave. It stood upright and was not held in place with other stones as many other tombstones were. They positioned it deep in the dirt and then stepped away to see how it looked.

On the stone, it read.

***Cornelius Antiochus***
***Centurion of Caesarea***
***Disciple of Yeshua***

The remaining eight men stared at the marker, embracing the finality of their leader's life. All of them stared at the ground and for the moment, they were oblivious to the cold. They had an unscripted moment of reflection as they pondered the complete silence that now came from this man no longer being with them. Caleb knew it was his job to speak first.

"I imagine my uncle already stands before Jehovah and has received answers to many of the questions that haunted him," said Caleb, staring at the dirt below. Caleb knew that his questions would be answered one day but for now, he drew solace from the truth that his uncle was now finding peace.

A few men let out a single chuckle. Then, another spoke up.

"I can see him smiling and nodding his head now that he understands the meaning of what it said in that one scroll to the Romans that he read all the time. He could not make sense of the fact that there is no condemnation for those who live in Yeshua the Messiah. How many times did we all hear him struggle with that? He condemned himself more than anyone I have known." That made everyone break eye contact with the dirt, look at each other, and laugh.

Finally, Matthew, Caleb's father-in-law, chimed in.

"I bet he has already found Simon Peter and asked where the hell he ran off to."

Hysterical laughter ensued. Caleb shook his head side to side as he realized that the loss Cornelius felt with Simon Peter was now also his to bear, as he would no longer have a great man to turn to for guidance when he hated himself or what was required of him. He, too, found the condemnation clause from the new Torah to feel like an unbelievable story. He felt rudderless and would need to spend some time with Mishi before the day ended. As he told his men, there was no better medicine than time with his firstborn.

All these men knew the real man who was now in the ground. He feared Yahweh. He tried to keep the law. He loved Yeshua's teachings of grace. Yet they knew he left this world before he found peace. There is no reconciliation between a man who held the job of a centurion and that of a disciple of Yeshua. Holding men accountable, killing them for their crimes, and extracting a fair share of taxes from the unwilling and the poor all stood in opposition to the Messiah's teachings of mercy and forgiveness. Caleb questioned if that claim was true.

"I am grateful that his struggles are now over and he has found peace," said Caleb. None of the men could see, though, that Caleb already was yearning for the same thing his uncle had just received. Caleb put his arm around the man next to him and began moving toward the gates, signifying the end of the moment.

"Men, let me have a few moments with my uncle. Please go with Val and offer her your condolences. I will be there soon," he said. The men bowed their heads, hugged him, and left, walking back to the property's central courtyard.

Caleb didn't take long to say his goodbyes. He knew his uncle had emptied himself as he prepared Caleb to be the centurion. All he had were words of gratitude and a promise to look to heaven for guidance.

Moments after everyone had left, Caleb joined them in the central courtyard of what was now his property. Inheritance transferred at the time of burial and now all that Cornelius owned was Caleb's.

Valentina spoke to Caleb as soon as he walked in.

"Caleb, I need to tell you this before we start serving food and offering up toasts. Your uncle and I decided many years ago that we would like to distribute three portions of our wealth evenly among the servants. Adi has already told us that she loves this idea and wants no portion for herself other than a few items from her father's study. You, Yael, and your cousin Eliza can keep the remaining portion for yourselves and Eliza's ministry. However, we wish to leave to you and Yael our home, water rights, and our spot at the pier. If you continue as the centurion, it makes good sense."

"OK. Thank you, Aunt Val. You know uncle already told me that, right?"

Caleb paused before he continued. He was unsure if the following words were appropriate or not.

"Aunt Val, I am not a fan of sailing across the sea, considering what happened the last time Eliza and I got on a boat," he said. Valentina smiled and touched the man on his chest as if he was a young man who didn't want to get up in the morning to walk to school. She was familiar with the peculiarities of prominent and influential men in the military who also had a soft side to them. Indeed, finding that spot and speaking to it is where her spiritual gifts were.

"If you are to take up your cross and bear it daily, you will sail, my boy. I assure you, you will sail. Your son will learn to sail, as will his sons. You don't think this is the first time I have heard some idiot of a centurion say that, do you?" she asked. Caleb laughed at the simplicity of her claims. He knew she was right.

She put two hands on his chest, looked up at him, and stared into his eyes. He had watched her do this to Cornelius and he knew that whatever she said next would flower in his heart.

"When the emperor calls, you must go. Yeshua will always go with you, even if your uncle no longer can," she said, looking him directly in the eye and awaiting his acknowledgment.

"OK," he finally said. He closed his eyes as more tears began to flow, and he embraced his aunt as if it were the last thing he would accomplish. After a moment, he stopped and looked down into her eyes.

"Auntie, when would you like me to tell everyone?"

"As soon as Eliza's eulogy is over. I have already told all the servants who are getting a share to stay after and speak with you. They know something but not everything that I have told you."

"OK. I have a job to give my men, and then I will take them to the basement once the meal ends."

Caleb knew his uncle had a vault below the kitchen for the earth's treasures, but Caleb had never been invited to the basement. His uncle's spoken words were worth more than gold, and the two of them seldom talked about personal wealth. Caleb knew that all of Cornelius' years of service to the Empire in a foreign land meant that he probably amassed several talents of gold and silver. Caleb and Yael speculated that their hardship allowance for living and working so far from Rome probably paid all their bills with much left over. Caleb and Yael had yet to spend even ten gold pieces since he began receiving a centurion's pay a few months ago, and they seldom saw Val spend money on anything other than paying the servant's salaries. He knew that whatever was down there must occupy a lot of shelf space.

"Here is the key to the vault, Caleb. Go with your cousin Eliza. There will be many things down there that she will want to see perhaps more than you do," she said. Caleb had no idea what she meant, but he trusted her and committed to speaking to Eliza as soon as they left.

The families of all seven servants had already entered the compound. They were offering their condolences to the family of the most remarkable man they had known. Nearly everyone cried at one point or another, and many people offered up remembrances of the man who ruled on behalf of the Roman Empire and Yeshua for almost half a century. Despite not having a funeral pyre, they did have to keep a large fire burning for everyone to stay warm and keep the stories flowing.

After telling Eliza about the basement, Caleb brought the funeral meal gathering to order. He stood at the end of the outdoor table where the ceremonial last meal would be served. He went to the end of the table and picked up the Elijah cup, which had been a local tradition for nearly a thousand years. He lifted it and spoke.

"To the man who replaced my father and guided my wife and I these last three years, I hope that I will replace him with honor. I lift this cup and bless my cousin Eliza as she delivers his eulogy."

Caleb set the cup down and stepped to the side to allow Eliza to stand in the middle and begin teaching.

"All of you know that Caleb's parents were also my aunt and uncle. They recorded this scroll and gave it to Cornelius and Valentina's now-deceased son, Rufus, many years ago. Since then, I am sure my uncle has read its words many times. I wish I could have been here to help him translate it and answer the questions this sacred scroll creates. I wish to read a small portion of it to you, as it is the story of Cornelius' teacher, Simon Peter. This is the story of his calling."

Caleb approached her, adorning her with his mother's ceremonial robe worn by priests who read the Torah. She covered her head with her prayer shawl and carefully removed the scroll from its protective case. She unfurled it to find the section she intended to read. Finally, she lifted her hands in reverent prayer before she began.

"This is the Word of Yahweh, as powerful and meaningful as the words given to Moses. May it be passed on to all future generations." Many people nodded in agreement. She looked around the room, formulating how she wanted to teach the contents of the story of Cornelius. She smiled as the idea took shape and she took a final deep breath before introducing them to her message.

"As you all know, Simon Peter, whom our uncle called Peter, came to this home many years ago." She paused for effect.

"Peter spoke with Cornelius for several days and perhaps some of you. His visit ended when he called all of this house to follow Yeshua. Let us start with the tale of the man before his visit. I will read the story of how Yeshua called Peter."

She smiled and looked down at the scroll. Caleb could see that she was excited to read. This was a longer reading, and she adjusted her prayer shawl before she began.

*"One day, Yeshua was standing by the Lake of Gennesaret. That is on the Sea of Galilee, where the people were crowding around him and listening to the word of Yahweh. He saw at the water's edge two boats left there by the fishermen who were washing their nets. He got into one of the boats, the one belonging to Simon, and asked him to put out a little from shore. Then he sat down and taught the people from the boat. When he had finished speaking, he said to Simon, 'Put out into deep water and let down the nets for a catch.' Simon answered, 'Master, we've worked hard all night and haven't caught anything. But because you say so, I will let down the*

*nets.' When they had done so, they caught such a large number of fish that their nets began to break. So they signaled their partners in the other boat to come and help them, and they came and filled both boats so full that they began to sink. When Simon Peter saw this, he fell at Yeshua' knees and said, 'Go away from me, Lord; I am a sinful man!' For he and all his companions were astonished at the catch of fish they had taken, and so were James and John, the sons of Zebedee, Simon's partners.*

*Then Yeshua said to Peter, 'Don't be afraid; from now on, you will fish for people.' So, they pulled their boats up on shore, left everything, and followed him."*

Everyone nodded. All of them had heard that story before. After a few more moments of teaching, Eliza changed scrolls.

"And this is the story of how Peter met our beloved Cornelius Antiochus." Eliza opened the newer scroll and let forth a slight chuckle that quickly turned to tears. This was the same handwriting she read when she was learning to read when she was three years old. She remembered spilling some tea on one of Aunt Yael's scrolls and how mad her aunt got when she learned Eliza brought food and set it next to the new Torah. She spanked Eliza and Uncle Mishi pointed a finger at her and told her not to do that again. And there, in the bottom left corner of the scroll, was the tea stain.

"I remember this scroll and the tea stain," she said. Eliza could not contain the impact of that memory and she wept. Caleb knew the tea story but no one else did. She looked up at him and he smiled and nodded to her. She needed him to do that; his nod meant that everything would be OK. She took a deep breath and then read the story. Everyone knew the story of Simon, the Tanner, the trip to Joppa, the return visit, and the outpouring of the Holy Spirit. Many said "Hallelujah" as she read, and she joyfully reached the end.

Once she was done, Eliza closed the scroll, looked up, and smiled. Everyone was again quiet, and she felt confident with what she intended to do next. Unlike her teacher, Dor, Eliza didn't need to practice her sermons in advance. The gift of words came naturally to her. It now was her time to use the power she gleaned from watching her aunt Yael unravel mysteries to crowds of hungry unbelievers looking to make sense of their ancient heritage with the remnants of a fallen temple that used to symbolize their faith.

She knew none of these servants knew they were about to inherit immense wealth. Before the sun set, they would be in the top one percent of all Caesarea residents in terms of net worth. She took a sense of responsibility, knowing these would be the last words they heard before they became rich.

More memories of her dead aunt Yael resurfaced at times like these. She remembered how her aunt would meet a beggar when they were working in the markets by the sea, and she would listen to the man, pray with him, and then give him whatever extra coins she had. She always found it interesting that her aunt did not give money to people asking for it. She exclusively gave it to people who didn't prioritize gathering wealth that way. She could see that her aunt and uncle were made from the same stew.

Eliza and Caleb were gifted linguists and fluent in many of the languages of faith and commerce. In addition to learning Greek and Ebreet, they knew Egyptian, Aramaic, and Farsi. She grew up managing coin and merchant trade, and her travels on the Silk Road with her father and uncle taught her the manipulation of currency and negotiation in commerce. People often said that she could sell sand to a camel. It was easy for Dor to appoint her as the treasurer of his ministry with a stern reminder not to follow Judas Iscariot. Yet her passion remained that of a teacher and counselor to those who are hurting and looking for a place to call home.

With all that in mind, she stepped away from the pedestal Caleb had set up for her, approached Caleb, and unsheathed his gladius. It weighed much more than she remembered, and she twisted it in her hands to look at both sides. Even though it was cold, the sun was directly overhead, and the sapphires and emeralds that encrusted the hilt glimmered as she spun the weapon.

"When Peter came to my uncle, we read that the Holy Spirit was already working in both men. Peter was one of us and knew the Torah. However, our uncle Cornelius was raised in Rome and led the people in Caesarea with a rudimentary understanding of the Torah. Cornelius and Valentina were members of the local synagogue and feared Yahweh, but there is no record that Peter knew how our Messiah was working in Cornelius."

She paused to make eye contact with some of the older men and women in the audience who were there when Peter arrived. They nodded in affirmation and she continued.

"Peter thought Cornelius was like all other Centurions, using blades such as this one. Peter probably thought that Cornelius and this blade were one and the same." She ran her finger along the edge and casually walked to the other side of the audience.

"To Peter, Cornelius and Valentina were steeped in the tradition of Rome and their Pagan gods. Peter knew that both Romans and Ebreet were persecuting early followers of Yeshua and he was concerned that he would also be taken away and killed. Our Lord saw Peter's heart and told him not to be afraid. Peter didn't know that Cornelius and Valentina were God-fearing and had already embraced Jehovah of Abraham, Isaac, and Jacob."

She gave Caleb back his blade and kissed him on the cheek. She returned to the pedestal and removed a different scroll, appearing to be reading the words. However, she wasn't looking at them; she was fidgeting. Her aunt used to fidget this way, too.

"Caleb's blade is a weapon of great power. I have seen him humble men to their knees with it and never swing it." She looked at Caleb and chuckled as everyone stared at her, wondering where she was taking this teaching.

"Don't you think that Peter must have been scared?" she asked the crowd without looking at any of them. She looked up and spoke at a much faster cadence.

"After all, he had seen evil things Roman leaders like Nero and Pilate did with his own eyes. Peter knew these people were capable of the worst possible acts. He saw his rabbi hung on a cross at Golgotha.

He saw Stephen get stoned. He saw countless beheadings. I am sure he could not forget that Rome meant death."

She again paused. Although she had not observed a crucifixion, she had heard her sister talk about how Caleb would come and completely shut down for days when he condemned men to death by this method. However, she intentionally avoided any eye contact with Caleb. She could not share his grief right now.

"The scrolls tell us how Peter responded. It says that Peter went to the roof of the building where he was staying. The roof serves many purposes, but it is always considered a safe place, away from threats."

She paused and turned her head to the side, looking inquisitively at the people in front of her.

"What kind of a response is that? His response to learning that men from a centurion were coming for him was to hide on a roof?"

She again showed the look of someone who doubted what they had just heard.

"If that isn't the action of a scared man, then I don't know fear!"

Eliza waited for a bit of laughter to subside before she continued. This was not her first time teaching this crowd, and it was evident that she was improving her delivery and insight.

"Did Peter not know that Yeshua remained with him as he traveled to Joppa? I assure you that Peter knew it in his mind, but it wasn't in his actions that day. Can we fault him? Have we not done the same thing in our lives, forgetting that the power of a risen Messiah lives inside of us? I have." Several older members nodded at her and she could tell that they were reliving the moment when Peter was with them.

"I say to you, none of us should be like Peter. However, we all are like Peter. Yeshua is among us, even now, carrying the weary soul of my uncle into Eternity."

She paused to adjust her robe and wipe tears from her eyes. Dor told her he could tell when the Holy Spirit was upon her, as she would feel no shame in crying while she taught.

"Although this tale is of someone dear to you, I hope you can see that this is the story of everyone. How many times have we been scared and hidden from our responsibilities? How often have we run to a roof when we know that we were called to embrace the enemy at the door and kiss him on the cheek?" Eliza paused to look at the audience and make eye contact with many of them.

"Peter knew men were coming for him and he knew how Yeshua would have stood outside to greet them as they approached. Yet he did no such thing. Instead, he went to the roof and waited. The scroll says he became hungry as well. That means he was there a long time!" She spoke her last sentence with emphasis and everyone began to laugh again.

"When the men finally found him, what did he say? Was he a Godly disciple of the Messiah, greeting them with a Shalom and kisses? Did he offer them a place to sit or a cup to drink?"

She paused again to look to the heavens.

"No! The scrolls say he spoke to them, asking, 'Why have you come for me?'" Eliza left her place next to the scrolls, walked into the audience, and stood near some of her uncle's most trusted servants. She got within arm's length of them before she continued teaching.

"No. That is a question asked by a man who was deeply concerned for his well-being. He did not greet them as he was taught and instead wanted to know his fate. He again showed little faith, just as he did at other places in this scroll of Acts," She walked to another family and looked at them.

"I remind you, this story is about the man who brought the Holy Spirit of this house. This scared little man became the mentor and hero of the man that my cousin now replaces," she said, pointing to Caleb.

"This man's teachings saved many of you from slavery at the hands of the Roman empire. It was this scared man that our God used to change the history of our faith and the history of everyone in this house." She raised her finger again and walked back to the scrolls.

"Yahweh had spoken to Peter repeatedly in a dream. Peter knew Yahweh was Emmanuel, Yahweh with us. Yet was it enough? No, he remained hungry and stayed on a roof with visitors soon to arrive.

Here is what it says." She unrolled the small section of scripture that she needed and read it out loud.

*"Upon arrival, Cornelius' men told him the one who sent them was a believer in Yahweh, and he was asked to come to this home in Caesarea and speak to him and his family. While Cornelius awaited Peter's arrival, he asked some of you and many of your parents to come and be present when Peter arrived."*

She looked up from her uncle's scroll, pausing for people to catch up to her.

"Perhaps some of you remember that moment? Perhaps some of you were here when Peter entered that gate over there?" She pointed to the gate and smiled. Several men and one woman raised their hands.

"We were there!" one of them said. Another one spoke up loudly.

"My older brother was one of the men who walked to Joppa and the house of Simon, the Tanner."

She looked around and saw others nodding with him. That man was proud of his brother's participation in recorded history.

"What do you remember hearing of his journey?" she asked. She knew that this man needed to talk and she gave him his share of this ceremony. He talked about the mystery of walking directly to the man's house without needing to ask directions to where Simon the Tanner lived. He said that finding Simon the Tanner's house in a city that neither had visited was a miracle.

"My brother told me stories about how all of them were filled with the Holy Spirit, but they didn't know what it was. Now, we know what that is," he said. She thanked him for sharing and continued her teaching.

"When Peter finally came to this place, some of you remember that God had already prepared a place for all of them. Peter explained the meaning of the teachings of the Messiah, and all believed. He spent time teaching other members of your synagogue down the hill." The house of worship that all these people attended was only a few minutes' walk down the stairs on this side of town.

"It is that man's efforts, the author of this scroll, the heart of Caleb, the love of my mother and sister, and the gifts Yahweh has given me that bring me in front of you today, speaking with authority that our heritage says no woman should have. I tell all of you, our Messiah's appearance changed everything!"

Every eye was glued to Eliza, none more than Caleb. Caleb was proud of his cousin's teaching ability and knew that his role as head of this household mandated that he publicly support her. He remembered his uncle's teachings on what to do in those moments.

"Boy, being a centurion includes acting like one when no one is telling you to! Place yourself next to the ones you support and show them that you care. Don't wait to be told. Just stand with them and your message will be heard. You don't need to say a damn thing. Just stand there."

Caleb knew it was time to show respect for his uncle's instructions. As such, he stepped forward and stood next to Eliza, letting her know that he was publicly there to support her. He placed his hands behind his back and bowed his head, showing his respect for the power of her words. Eliza smiled, nodded back, and continued.

"I have a challenge for all of you. You know from our people's history that the duty is upon the next generation to teach about the Exodus, Genesis, the law of Moses, and our place as Yahweh's chosen people. However, I also call all of you to teach the story of the Messiah. This story is more important than perhaps any other. Indeed, I have committed my life to teach it."

As her last act in this eulogy, she reached over and picked up the Elijah cup, lifting it over her head. The gasping of air made it feel like everyone had stopped breathing. Caleb's eyes bulged as she lifted a ceremonial cup that no woman had held in this household before now.

She looked down to compose herself before she looked up and spoke.

"This is the Elijah cup. It is meant for the Messiah. He has come and now lives in me and within you. It is now our cup. You, too, may drink from this cup if you allow Yeshua to live in you," she said. She took a drink from it and handed it to Caleb to drink from as well. Caleb reverently submitted to Eliza's request, took a sip, and took it from Eliza.

"Centurion, share with our family the blood of the Messiah," she said. Caleb began walking around in the crowd, offering a drink to anyone who wanted it. Not everyone took a drink, but many did. Once he was done, Caleb returned the cup to Eliza and took his place next to her. Eliza thanked him, set the cup down, and continued her lesson.

"Caleb has been my protector since I was a little girl and we went to school together. He is my leader and my warrior. He is now our centurion and I publicly submit to him in all things."

She adjusted her head covering and knelt before Caleb. Caleb placed his hand upon her head, signifying that he accepted her act of reverence and that she should stand back up. He put his right hand on the left side of her face and smiled.

Everyone understood this act of fealty. They knew it would expected of them. However, Eliza knew that there was more story to tell if these people were to be sincere in their submission to Caleb and Yael as the heads of this city.

"Yes, Caleb is now our leader, but there is a story you should know, as it will help you best understand our family and who now stands in front of you."

She broke eye contact and nodded for Yael to come forward and stand next to Caleb. Once she did, she stood in front of them and spoke loudly.

"Many of you know that Roman soldiers killed Caleb's parents. I watched as Caleb struck down a centurion trying to protect me."

She paused to allow a few quiet words to be shared in the crowd. A few knew that Caleb had killed other Romans. She raised her voice and continued.

"Now, my cousin Caleb is himself a centurion. He is *our* centurion. How can this be without grace?"

She quickly turned to face Yael and put a hand on her shoulder.

"This is my sister, Yael. Yael was raped by a member of the house of Caesar who paid nothing for his crime."

She paused. Although she was ashamed to discuss it openly, she had already asked and received permission from Yael to discuss it with the extended family. They needed to know that if they were to bend the knee to these two for the rest of their lives.

"Now, the ring on her finger signifies her as a member of house Caesar. Perhaps she is the most powerful woman in all of Manasseh. How can this be without grace?"

She moved to place herself between the two of them.

"And this woman is married to this man! They have a beautiful baby boy who has already received a prophecy, and she carries another in her womb. How is this possible?"

She held her sister's hand and looked again at the crowd, changing her tone to change how her following words would be received.

"These two are the epitome of what grace looks like."

Eliza needed to compose herself before she could speak the following sentence.

"These two people are my heroes. You should bend your knee and allow them to be yours."

Eliza could feel the Holy Spirit traversing through her veins. The transition from Cornelius to Caleb as head of household was nearly complete. Without exception, everyone in attendance was mesmerized by what she shared. Many in the crowd were already crying and kneeling to receive Caleb's touch.

"I tell you the truth: You all should see and believe that our Messiah can use all things for the good of those who live in the promise of our Messiah. All things include rape, the murder of parents, crucifixions, and death itself." She paused to see heads nod.

"I serve Yeshua and his message. These two are followers of Yeshua and are now your leaders within the Empire. They will always have my support and I will always support them. Will you support them?" she asked.

All of them went down to their knees in reverence, showing their support.

"I challenge you; where will you walk now that Cornelius is not here? Will you stay on the line he showed you or will you wander?" She knew that nearly none of them knew how much inheritance they were about to receive, and she knew that this question needed to linger and be the last one she asked them.

Caleb and Yael walked through all the servants, and he placed his hand on each one, accepting their act of fealty. Once they did, they each stood up and kissed Yael on the cheek, as is tradition, calling each of them "Your Grace". Once all of them had submitted, Eliza ended the funeral with a prayer, and people walked to the other side of the courtyard to Valentina's table to begin eating. What happened next would change them for generations.

# Chapter 5:
# Hanging the Signs

After the meal ended, Eliza dismissed the guests and servants who were not to receive an inheritance. While the women accepted condolences, Caleb pulled aside his five lieutenants and the servants who had been loyal to Cornelius. He took them off to the side and had them form a semi-circle around him. He stood straight with his hand on his sword's hilt, speaking to them with authority.

"Men, my uncle trained and trusted all of you. As such, I will trust you until you damage my trust. The first task I wish for you to do is hang these two signs. One should be installed at the bottom of the stairs above the entrance to my home, and the other should go above the gate leading into this city from the new Jerusalem Road. Take down the signs that bear his name, as he did not want that. The hell with what the Senate told us to do!"

The men nodded in agreement, and they carried the two large signs leaning against the compound's stone walls and set them outside the gates. They were made of bronze and required two people each to carry them. Caleb spoke to them after they set them down. The bigger message he must deliver is the next one.

"Unlike Cornelius, I am from Benjamin and was raised by two rabbis, not unlike my cousin Eliza. I know the God of Abraham, Isaac, and Moses. She told you the truth that both of my parents were killed by soldiers who looked much like you." He looked down and kicked a little of the dust at his feet before continuing.

"What you just heard was true. In my rage and efforts to protect Eliza, I killed several of those men and their centurion," the men looked at each other in shock.

"You may find this hard to believe, but the person who trained me to kill effectively was Cornelius' son, Rufus."

He paused to let the impact of that information begin to set in. Everyone there had heard of Rufus and the older servants knew him when he was a powerful young man, but none of his lieutenants had met him. The look on their face displayed shock that he would openly tell them of a capital crime that he had committed many years earlier. Caleb and his uncle agreed that this was not something that Caleb would tell his leadership until the transfer of authority between Cornelius and Caleb was complete. Cornelius knew their respect for him was contingent on proof that he knew how to fight and kill.

"I, too, and a Roman soldier, just like you. You have already heard the story that I have been to Rome and fought in the Coliseum as a gladiator against seasoned foes. The emperor watched the battle and appointed me a centurion shortly afterward." They all knew that, and Cornelius routinely bragged to his men about Caleb's prowess with a bow. Cornelius had shown his men the letter the emperor had written to him many years ago, which appointed Caleb. However, Caleb knew that telling them this truth allowed them to believe his claim and accept it. Caleb learned this skill with the timing of words from Rufus, and he began to wonder if Rufus didn't learn it from his father.

"Most importantly, I am a follower of Yeshua, just like my uncle and aunt before me. My cousin is the teacher in this family, and I am the warrior and soldier. However, when she speaks, she speaks for both of us. Eliza has a scroll of the prophets that discussed a transfer of leadership from Moses to the people who first crossed over into this land we now call Judah. A man named Joshua was deemed King after conquering these lands and the quote you see on those signs came from him. Trajan, go back to the sign and read those words out loud," pointing to the one they had just set down.

Trajan had an excellent memory. He didn't need to go back to remember what it said.

"It says, 'As for me and my house, we will serve Jehovah'."

"Good. As long as you remember the words on this sign, hold me accountable to them as I govern these people. My uncle told me I could trust you. So, I tell you, if you see that I am not serving the Lord with my efforts, bring it to my attention. Understood?" he ended with an authoritative tone that he learned from his uncle.

David was one of the youngest lieutenants and he looked at Caleb.

"Of course, we understand you, but what do we do if you aren't serving Jehovah?"

"Good question. Look me in the eye and tell me that. Remind me of this moment. Remind me that I trust you."

"Centurion, I speak for all of us. We know you care for the people here, and we all want to do that with you. You have earned our trust," he said.

"David, the way to see that I am a good man is how I treat my wife. I must be willing to lay down my life for her and our children. I need to be that man and I need to show you how to be that man as one day, you, too, will have a wife and a family. If I am not doing that, you will know."

"Centurion, I also want that," he said.

"We shall pray for the Lord to send you a woman, then!" Caleb said, striking the man on the back of his leather jerkin. Everyone laughed and Caleb dismissed them all.

# Chapter 6:
# Distribution of Wealth

With his senior leadership now busy hanging two signs, Caleb returned to his family and completely removed all of his military apparel. He came back out from his and Yael's bedroom, and Val was waiting for him. She leaned into him and he could feel her hands shaking. The gravity of losing the person she had traveled life with was starting to show. She was an old woman and losing strength. She was finding it difficult to stand on her own. The servants gathered at the banquet were saddened to see Val in that state, and some of them began to weep. Val addressed the group.

"Don't mind an old woman who just lost her best friend." She looked at Eliza and Yael, motioning them to come to her. Val was frightened watching all the people come and go from her home today, and she needed to feel Eliza and Yael's touch. Eliza took her place next to Val and inhaled deeply, smiling at the servants and their families. Once Val appeared to stabilize, Eliza spoke to her as a counselor.

"We are all here, Aunt Val. No one is leaving you," she said.

"Take them to the basement. You know what is about to happen," said Val. Val knew she was raised in a village with a gold mine; she knew how people behaved when vast wealth passed in front of them. And whether she admitted it or not, she loved moments like these when the power of gold was on display. She let out a single chuckle, knowing that she was trained for this next job, but she was not expecting it.

"Caleb, can you please give me the key?" Eliza said. She took off her prayer robes and shawl and removed the silver needle that held her thick brown hair up. She shook her head to let her hair down. Caleb handed her the key, and she opened the door.

"Cornelius and Val have decided to pass most of their inheritance to you. Send at least one person from each household with me to the basement. You are all about to become rich." Eliza didn't make eye contact with anyone; she walked down the stairs.

Each family sent one person down the dried mud steps. Val had asked Yael to go down and light a few candles earlier in the day, and it was easy for them to follow the path. Once everyone reached the bottom of the stairs, Eliza faced the seven representatives.

"I can't see anything. Please get some more candles and come back down," she said. As the first servant turned to walk away, a different one stepped up and held their arm, signaling them to stop.

"No, wait. There is a small window at the top of the back wall that the master would open when he came here to read and write. Let me open it for you," he said. He didn't wait for Eliza's permission but reached up to the hidden wooden plank that covered the window and opened it. Immediately, the room was lit up enough for all to see.

"I had no idea," said Caleb. He looked at Eliza and nodded his head in wonder. He looked around the room and saw all of Cornelius' wealth for the first time. This place was more than just a family vault. In addition to storing the family gold, silver, bronze, copper, diamonds, emeralds, rubies, and sapphires, there was a table and two chairs in the middle of the room. Next to the table were two large shelves filled with parchment and scrolls. There was an inkpot and several pens, as well.

"This was also his library and study!" said Eliza, looking at Caleb with the joy of discovery on her face.

"Another one of uncle's secrets!" said Caleb. The servant who opened the window spoke next.

"The master would come down here in the mornings when all were asleep. He would come up as soon as he heard footsteps in the kitchen and send me down here to close whatever he was working on." Eliza nodded as she began to understand the puzzle. She wondered who else knew about this place.

"Well, I had no idea our uncle was such a prolific writer! He did not talk to me about it. Regardless, I am glad that you knew about that window. With all these scrolls down here, I don't like the idea of having candles burning alongside them," said Eliza, bringing laughter from nearly everyone. She waited for the laughter to stop before she continued with the explanation of why they were all in this little room. She motioned for Caleb to slide the shelf that contained all the precious metals and gems toward the table and center.

"My uncle and aunt wish to give you and your families most of their wealth. Caleb, Yael, and I are very happy for you. But don't worry about us; we are getting some of it, too!" she said. The light-hearted nature of her comments allowed some of the freedom to cry some tears of joy as their years of living like every other Ebreet was now over. They could now afford any home they wanted and pay for their children to have lavish weddings and travel to Rome to go shopping. Once their conversation settled a bit, Eliza continued in her role as treasurer.

"I will now count the coins and jewels in front of you. You all are about to become very rich. How does that sound?" she asked. She knew that this would ignite some of their greed, and she preferred that it be exposed when friends were around to help them diffuse it. All of them clapped and a few of them hugged each other, telling themselves that they deserved it.

Caleb lifted and poured the first chest of silver coins on the tabletop to a round of applause. The coins covered nearly all of the table. Caleb started with silver because it was, by far, the most valuable of all the precious metals during the time of the Roman Empire. Eliza gave everyone a single coin, almost like it was a sample of food at the docks on Yom Kippur. Then, she stacked all the coins into seven piles. Next, Caleb poured out the gold, then the bronze, and finally the copper. Eliza had him do it in that order, as she wanted to give them the best of their inheritance first. The speed at which she counted the coin made it evident that she had counted this wealth many times before, and she showed no emotion as she moved enough money to buy a small village or an island off the coast.

"What questions do you all have?" she asked as she stacked the coins into equal piles for each family. She couldn't answer many of their questions about how long all of this had been down here, but she remained focused on completing the allocations as quickly as she could.

Once the coins were done, she removed the precious stones and intricate jewelry and placed them in piles. Some families chimed in, as the value of a silver necklace was ambiguous, and she waited for all families to agree before moving forward with the rest.

Once she finished, she announced out loud that each family would receive four minahs of silver coins. One minah was their standard pay for one year of labor. The amounts of gold were nearly the same. She dared not to count the amount of copper, as it was, by far, the biggest and was the most commonly used coin type at the marketplace. There was also a large pouch full of gems for each family, perhaps worth more than all the coins. Each family extended thanks, and she graciously accepted on behalf of Cornelius and Valentina.

Finally, she took the share meant for Caleb and Yael and put it back in the chest, along with small pouches for each kind of gem.

"Caleb, that belongs to you and my sister. Since she is not here, please take this upstairs and show it to her. She is busy with your son. It is the least you could do." she said.

"Yes, cousin," he said, speaking in the same tone that one of the servants might use. Eliza knew what he was doing as she had been there when Cornelius repeatedly taught him how to behave.

"Lead by example, boy. If you want them to submit, you must also submit," his now-dead uncle would say. Once Caleb reached the top of the stairs and the room was quiet, Eliza spoke.

"My uncle knew that this day would give all of you temporary happiness and a feeling of peace. However, he also knew that it would be a day when the evil one would attempt to enter your heart and convince you to discard the law of Moses. Our Messiah did not abolish the law, as some are led to believe. He completed it."

She paused to look at them before she continued.

"But first, I will tell you a story." She could tell they were anxious so she shortened the tale.

> *"A man of noble birth went to a distant country to be appointed king and then to return. So he called ten of his servants and gave them ten minas. 'Put this money to work,' he said, 'until I come back.' But his subjects hated him and sent a delegation after him to say, 'We don't want this man to be our king.' He was made king, however, and returned home. Then he sent for the servants to whom he had given the money to find out what they had gained with it. The first one came and said, 'Sir, your mina has earned ten more.' 'Well done, my good servant!' his master replied. 'Because you have been trustworthy in a tiny matter, take charge of ten cities.' The second came and said, 'Sir, your mina has earned five more.' His master answered, 'You take charge of five cities.' Then another servant said, 'Sir, here is your mina; I have kept it in a piece of cloth. I was afraid of you because you are a hard man. You take out what you did not put in and reap what you did not sow.' His master replied, 'I will judge you by your own words, you wicked servant! You knew, did you, that I am a hard man, taking out what I did not put in and reaping what I did not sow? Why didn't you put my money on deposit so that when I came back, I could have collected it with interest?' Then he said to those standing by, 'Take his mina away from him and give it to the one who has ten minas.' 'Sir,' they said, 'he already has ten!' He replied, 'I tell you that to everyone who has, more will be given, but as for the one who has nothing, even what they have will be taken away."*

Once she finished, she made eye contact with nearly everyone present before speaking.

"What did that story mean to you?" she asked.

She knew that none would answer her quickly. Instead, she refocused the question.

"I see you staring at each of the piles. You know you will get one of them with no conditions on what you do with it. That means you now have more wealth than anyone you know. Do you think it is your master's intention for you to spend it or grow it?" This time, she expected an answer. One of the men who lived with his family on the compound spoke first. He was always a talker while Cornelius was his master.

"Spend some and invest some, rabbi. I will use some of these coins to host my daughter's wedding and give some to her new husband. However, I intend to invest the rest and see it grow, so I have some for my other two daughters," he said. Eliza knew that if she wanted others to share, she needed to affirm this man's answer.

"Our uncle would be pleased with your choices! Well done!" Eliza looked the man in the eyes and nodded her approval. Dor had taught her that one of the greatest gifts a rabbi offers is approval when she finds a student who understands when she teaches.

One older woman servant who was recently widowed decided to share.

"I have no intentions today. Perhaps I will give some to the synagogue," she said.

Eliza nodded her approval.

"I will make it grow, as there are no needs that I have that our master and his wife did not meet for me," said another servant. That one made Eliza smile. She affirmed his choice and heard her sister and her baby coming down the stairs. Eliza ignored everyone else for a moment and asked why Yael had come downstairs.

"Uncle took me down here before I gave birth. He used to teach me to reach and write Greek and Ebreet in the mornings when the baby was restless inside of me, and I could not sleep," she said. Eliza looked at her with amazement, as she had no idea.

"I didn't know you wanted to learn," Eliza said in disbelief.

"Yes. He said I was a good student," she said. Yael looked down to finish formulating her thoughts, then looked up at her sister. All the servants were looking at the two sisters interact, but Yael didn't care. She needed to say this.

"Eliza, you sometimes made me feel stupid because I couldn't read and write Greek and Ebreet as well as you can," she said.

Another secret was now revealed.

"Yael, I am so sorry. I didn't," she said, but she got cut off.

"You wait. It is my turn to talk. Uncle heard me say this one time and he said that one of the last things he would do was teach me these languages. Uncle was a good teacher. I have read a couple of the scrolls he has set aside for you already. They have your name on them." Eliza didn't know what she was talking about, but she looked and continued her apology.

"I am so sorry, honey," Eliza said.

"I am glad that he brought me down here to teach me. He couldn't have picked a better tool to use than these scrolls, as I knew he intended to give them to you when he died," she said, pointing to the ones near her.

"What? Those are for me?" Eliza asked. Another secret was revealed. Yael didn't respond but pointed to them and nodded.

"Let's talk more about this later. I am giving the servants all of their money," Eliza said, easing everyone out of the awkwardness of the interaction between the two sisters. She repeated her question to the crowd.

"Who else wants to share their intentions?" Eliza asked.

"I will take my family to visit Jerusalem and see where the Temple used to be," said another servant who had patiently waited his turn. He was one of the two servants who carried the heavy items from the city below up the stairs to the compound. Yael was now sitting on the bottom stairs, feeding baby Mishi, and she added to the conversation.

"I remember traveling to the old city to find my parents a few years ago. I wonder what the ancient city looks like now. Uncle Cornelius would like that idea," she said. With that, it was time to give away the wealth.

"Come forward, one family at a time, and take your share of the inheritance. All these piles are all the same, so you can take anyone you wish."

Once the last of the coins and jewelry were distributed, Eliza turned to the group.

"No matter your choice, I encourage all of you to continue leading your lives as if my uncle was alive and able to speak to you. Remember that although he is not here, he would want you to make decisions that bring glory to Yeshua and not just your family. Understood?" she said.

"Yes, rabbi," that all repeated.

# Chapter 7:
# Introduction to the
# Scrolls of Cornelius

Eliza watched as everyone carried their precious coins and gems up the stairs, and she could hear their giddy screams as they left the compound to go down into the city. Once the last of them were gone, Eliza paused to look around at all that was left. There must have been a thousand scrolls of ancient books in different places on floors, shelves, and stairs. All had scripts and art stacked upon them, and there were tapestries and ancient relics on a shelf on one wall. Eliza walked up to one of them and picked it up.

"This candlestick looks just like the one my aunt showed me at the old woman's house outside of Jerusalem when I was a little girl." She knew it must have been a part of the Holy of Holies inside the Temple of King Solomon from twenty years ago.

"How did Uncle Cornelius get these?" she rhetorically asked as she ran her hand on an ancient tapestry hanging on the south wall. She took a candle out from the wall and examined it more closely. The tapestry depicted the Exodus from Egypt, and Moses stood with his hand on his staff as he extended it over the Sea of Reeds.

"The parting of the sea!" she said. She held the candle close to Moses and studied his hair, beard, cloak, sandals, and the men who stood nearby. He had been depicted as a simple man who had not been groomed in years.

"Caleb will look like that when he is an old man," she said as she laughed to herself. She told herself she needed to come back here when she had the time and considered that she might use some of these writings to teach her future disciples.

"If God wants me to call Romans to follow, I will need images like this to teach them the Torah," she said. After a few moments, she turned and went upstairs to join everyone else.

Eliza went into the kitchen to spend some time with her family. She knew Caleb had something to do at work and their father went with him, but she knew they would return quickly. For now, it was a girl-only gathering. She entered mid-conversation and quickly told them about the tapestry on the walls. Yael acted like she knew all about it and she offered Eliza a seat next to her. Val restarted the conversation now that Eliza had joined them.

"This little cooking fire has heard more stories than all the books in the great library in Alexandria," Val said.

"Or your basement! Aunt Val, there must be a thousand scrolls and books down there." Eliza took off her sandals and sat next to Yael. Her mother sat across from her and was telling her sister about a new section of road they were making in Correae. Soon, there would be a second route in and out of town. Eliza told Val about one of the Gaza landowners who supported Eliza's ministry and how his wife had borne him 12 children. The conversation was light and Val didn't want it to end. It was the perfect medicine for her grief.

"Honey, bring me the rest of Corn's whiskey," Val said. Yael brought the flask over with a small amount in four different golden chalices. Val told them to drink a small sip, wait a moment, and then drink the other sip. Katya had never had whiskey before and it burned as it went down, making all of them laugh. Yael filled everyone's cup a second time with what was left; then she added water to fill it to the top. She didn't want any of them to get drunk but only loosen their tongues.

Certainly, there was a lot of cleanup to be done but for now, whiskey was the better alternative. The girls talked about some of the antics of the deceased and soon, they were laughing continuously. Caleb returned and he carried Mishi in a pack on his back. He handed the hungry little boy back to his mother and sat next to everyone while his mother prepared to feed him. He politely refrained from the offer for a cup of whiskey and suggested that his wife get his portion. Yael got everyone's attention and spoke up.

"There is something else for each of us. Uncle has left us scrolls as part of our inheritance, and he asked me to make sure we read this one first together," she said, holding up the small roll of parchment in her left hand. She was breastfeeding her child and could do nothing more than hand it to Eliza to read. She continued talking as she gave it to her sister. She could read the look of shock on her sister's face.

"No, Eliza, I haven't read this scroll, but I would prefer if you could read it to all of us here, in the kitchen, and not down in the basement," she said. Everyone nodded in agreement. Val pulled fresh bread from the oven and brought up some dried meat from the food cellar. Once Val had sat back down, Eliza broke the seal and read it out loud.

> *Dear Caleb, Yael, and Eliza,*
>
> *If you are reading this, it means that this disease in my lungs has got the best of me, and I have gone home to be with the Messiah. I asked that you be together when you read this, as you have shown resilience in acting as one unit when life is difficult. Val and I agreed that you would soon need each other again like you did in the coliseum. I see a wind of change coming in Rome and have already been given visions that you will be part of it. I was given a vision that the children of the people whom you will call disciples will change the world. I also saw all of you in Rome one day soon, watching the humblest of people you have loved and cared for take positions of unfathomable power, and they will look to you for guidance. Be humble, and be with each other until this happens.*

Eliza's heart raced. This sounded like the rabbi in Calabria from three years earlier, right after their ship ran aground. Nightmares about that day haunted her and Yael told her just yesterday that Caleb continues to speak with others about that wreck and how mysterious their meeting with that rabbi felt.

"I respect uncle, but I don't want to go back to Rome," said Eliza. Everyone there already knew that she hated Rome more than anywhere else in the world. Yael pointed back at the scroll.

"Eliza, keep reading, please," she pleaded. Yael had been thinking about what might be in this scroll for the last few months when Cornelius showed it to her. Her anticipation came out in her tone.

> *As you know, Val and I spent most of our evenings alone, outside on the rooftop, connecting and sharing. Over the years, I have learned that I can share nearly all things with her, but not all things. Caleb, when you arrived, I found that I finally had someone with whom I could share everything. Val told me that she had nearly the same experience with Yael. The two of you living with us allowed both of us to release some of our greatest burdens and secrets. Indeed, your family was the most incredible blessing either of us had during our last days together.*
>
> *Eliza, it was wise of you to listen to Rabbi Dor's calling to follow him. I am sure you will be an influential priestess in our faith, and Dor will teach you much about the world's ways. Indeed, young lady, one of my letters for you to read is a copy of one I wrote to Dor a few years ago when he worked for me.*

"Hmm," Eliza said, looking at the wall to ponder what she had read. She sensed that there was a history between two of her favorite men; now she knew.

"It will not be surprising if these scrolls are not Cornelius' most valuable gift, perhaps more than the wealth." She looked at Caleb and smiled.

"Eliza, I didn't know that uncle knew Dor!" said Caleb. Val laughed. She obviously knew more than any of them.

> *Little One, it was in my dreams that I saw you discipling others as your aunt did. Instead, I will only watch you from eternity to the extent that Yahweh allows me. Although I will not get to see you in action in this life, I am sure you spoke at my funeral and left a permanent mark on everyone in attendance.*

Eliza looked up at her mother.

"Did I?" she asked, wiping a tear from her eye.

"I would say that the stones were listening to you," said Katya as she breastfed her child. Everyone looked at Katya and nodded their heads in agreement. Eliza thanked her mother and continued to the next section of the scroll.

> *Val and I have been praying most uniquely for you three, and she felt led to tell me to re-read and organize all my old writings in the basement. She suggested I pick out some of the more important ones and give them to each of you. Neither of us wants you to make the same mistakes that we did when we were young.*
>
> *For you, Caleb, I say this: Proving yourself within the Roman military is a full-time job, and seeking approval from your fellow soldiers and officers will cause you great pain. I hope you can look above this and perhaps see that Titus was wise in promoting you to a high position, so you don't need to worry about getting the approval of others.*
>
> *Boy, you have an excellent salary! Val and I think you need to embrace the truth that you do not need to earn more than a centurion earns. We pray you do not fall victim to the temptation to extort*

*from shopkeepers and merchants; we both know you will be tempted. It is our prayer that you can learn from me.*

*By now, you have learned that we gave Caleb and Yael our mountaintop estate. From here, you can see the city that you will govern below. In addition to the estate, we have taken some gold, silver, rubies, and sapphires and made them into jewelry to remember us. We have decided that each of you shall get a ring and a silver charm for your necklaces bearing both the Ebreet and Greek Letters for Centurion. Whoever wears this shall be considered family to the house of the Centurion in Caesarea. This shall afford you some protection as you embrace the difficulties coming your way. We ask that each time you have a moment when you remember these ornaments, you offer up a prayer that you help those in need. Use this as a reminder to rescue those being taken off to death and those stumbling toward slaughter.*

She turned, unrolled the last section of the scroll, and continued.

*The scrolls I now give you are the last part of our estate. They are not part of my Torah, nor should they be held in that regard. I spent about a month reading all of them as my body was fading. I have picked out some for each of you. They are not examples of my best days but represent some of the best lessons on my worst days. In that sense, they are much like the stories in the Torah. Eliza, I know you have your mother's rendition of what happened when Simon Peter arrived. I think you need to hear my perspective as well. That scroll is meant to be shared with as many people as you can.*

Eliza stopped reading but didn't look up. She pondered the depth of the last paragraph before letting out a small sound of approval before continuing.

> *May Yeshua help you find peace in your soul in ways that eluded me. I go to the grace as a wounded and unhealed man. I hope to awake in paradise with a new soul that no longer carries the burdens of Rome or this world. Take care of Val until she comes to me.*

Eliza allowed the scroll to roll itself back up and she tied it with the same piece of string that held it before she opened it. Underneath it were five originally signed copies of a small but royal decree, complete with the royal seal of house Flavian. It read,

> *By royal decree, I certify that anyone in possession of the jewels of the house of the Centurion of Caesarea is granted all the rights of Roman citizenship and royalty. They have full access to all property owned by the Empire and the freedom to act as they deem necessary to expand our great empire.*
> *-Domitian Flavian, Emperor of Rome*

Once Eliza finished reading the decree, she put it back down and wiped another handful of tears from her eyes.

"Are we all getting another ring? I can't escape these things," she said, giving everyone a cause for a well-needed laugh. A few years ago, Titus himself gave her a ring that made her a member of the family Caesar.

"Yes, and they are beautiful," said Yael. It was obvious that she had already known that part. She took out a small box of Lebanese cedar inlaid with gold, placing it in the center of the table where they all sat. Eliza spoke up.

"Wow. That box alone is worth half a year's wages." Yael handed her baby to Eliza and reached for the box.

"Now I can finally open this," she said. Yael opened it and saw that there were seven rings of different sizes as well as several charms. One ring was large and meant for Caleb. Two were smaller and meant for Yael and Eliza. Finally, there were four little ones. Her eyes opened to their fullest extent when she saw the four smaller ones. She didn't tell any of them that she had already seen the rings for Caleb, Eliza, and herself.

She looked at Caleb with a blend of concern and wonder.

"How long ago did you tell uncle that you wanted four children?" asked Yael.

"Perhaps two weeks, I don't know?" said Caleb. It was obvious to everyone that those were meant for their children and had recently been added to the box's contents.

"Well, he heard you," she said. The emotion of the day was now upon her and Yael began to cry again. After a moment, she took a deep breath and continued speaking. The baby was now asleep in Eliza's arms and she rocked it. She faced her sister and shared a thought she had carried for several days.

"Earlier today, you were talking to all of us about destiny through the story of Simon Peter. Now you are the recipient of your own teaching! It appears to be your destiny to wear a ring of membership at the highest levels in the Empire. Caleb?" She said, prompting him to act.

Caleb followed his queue as head of household. He walked behind his cousin, took off the necklace she received a few years earlier from her parents, and opened the clasp in the back. He added one of the charms Corn and Val had made for them to her necklace. As he slid it down the exquisite chain, he smiled and nodded. His uncle knew he would do this act and the jewel perfectly matched what Caleb's lifelong playmate was already wearing. He reclasped it and turned her around, looking at it. Yael spoke up.

"Eliza, I had no idea they were adding to our necklaces. About two months ago, Aunt Val asked me if I would take off my necklace so she could have it cleaned in the market. She had it for a few days before she gave it back. I think I know what she was doing now."

Caleb nodded as he remembered his wife telling him that story a few months ago. They all looked at Val and she just winked at them.

Caleb then did the same thing with his wife, adding the amulet to her necklace, identical to the one his cousin wears. Once he was done, he also slid the ring of the house of the centurion onto her finger. Yael looked down at it.

"I now have an amulet from my adopted father, my biological father, mother, and uncle," she said. The weight of the loss of her uncle and the thoughtfulness he displayed was now too much for all of them, and the group began crying deep tears. Once the sobbing stopped, Caleb broke the mood with another act his uncle would expect him to do.

"All of them had excellent taste in jewelry, cousin," said Caleb. Caleb took his larger silver hoop and slid it on the index finger of his sword hand, as is the tradition of Roman leadership.

Eliza sat up and Yael handed Caleb and Eliza their scrolls.

"OK, you two. Here are two of the scrolls that Uncle said are yours." She took out one more.

"Eliza, this is the one that he said you should share with everyone," and she handed him that one. It was on browner paper than the others, probably to make it stand out.

"I have already read one of mine. He said we should talk about them once we read them. Why don't the two of you go and read one? Let's see what uncle left for us."

Eliza took the largest scroll with her name on the outside, looked up, and hesitated. Then, she spoke.

"I am not yet ready to do this today, but I will start with the biggest scroll tomorrow. In the morning, mom and I planned to go shopping at the docks. I will take it with me and read it then." She put it back down on the table exactly where she had found it.

"I will go to the roof right now and read mine. I need a distraction," said Caleb.

"Good. I will stay here and reread mine," said Yael.

"Can I stay down here with you and the baby?" said Eliza.

"I was hoping you would say that," she responded.

# Chapter 8:
# To Caleb on earning the admiration of my superiors.

Caleb was anxious. He spent nearly every day of his life during these last three years with Cornelius, and he knew nothing about scrolls, letters, and stories from long ago hidden away in the basement. He held the document with his name on it and looked at it as he walked up the stairs to the quiet place on the roof where he would go to spend time away from everything. He couldn't tell how old the document was, but there was dust on the string that held it closed.

"This hasn't seen the light of day in a long time," he told himself as he reached the rooftop.

"OK, uncle. You told me to trust God in all things, but you have me wondering why you withheld this until you were dead and gone," he said out loud. No one was with him, but he had learned that hearing his voice gave him the ability to see if his thinking was that of a crazy man.

He laughed as he untied the string. He knew what his uncle would be telling him now.

"Boy, be brave. Just because you don't know what something is doesn't mean you shouldn't be friendly. An attitude of 'separation until safety' leads a man to live a lonely life. Open the door for someone you don't know. Greet that stranger coming down the docks you have never met. Talk to someone in the market you don't know. Get the hell out of your superiority mindset because you have the damn rank of a centurion! Be like the Son of God, and life will work out," Cornelius would say.

He unfurled the old parchment, which was written in Cornelius' hand. Based on the date, it was over 40 years old, and based on its contents, it predated his marriage to Aunt Valentina.

"Guard my heart, Yeshua," he said as he took a deep breath and started reading. He suspected it was a diary entry from his early days in the military. Now was the time to find out and stop speculating.

*"My men and I have been sent to Romanize the province of Hispania. There are reports of tribes of people from Turdetani attacking Roman cargo ships that sail through Gibraltar. The emperor told our Legion to do whatever was necessary to convince the men to submit to our authority. These 'people', if that is the right word for them, infested all the land on the right side of the boat as we sailed toward Gibraltar. None of them were intelligent enough to learn the language of Rome. Nearly all the villages and ports in Iberia to the East could speak with us, and they all taught our language in their schools, but these pseudo-people in Malaka[1] and Gadir[1] had troubled hearts and would not submit to us. We were sent to their shores to fix their views on our authority.*

*We picked up a translator in Abdera and exchanged our Roman cruisers for smaller ships that could land on the rocky coasts easily. We hope these vessels will help us find the leader of these rogue villages and explain to him that their land has been annexed and they are now a part of Rome. Submission to the emperor was non-negotiable, even though many thought it might be. Fools.*

*We carried a large sack of recently minted gold coins and we intended to have the translator tell them that they could use this sack to pay their first year of taxes so that it wouldn't cause them any hard-ships or political problems during their first season as part of the empire. We tried to explain that these coins would give them time to adjust to the modern world of paying taxes and receiving public services.*

*Concurrently, our Legate promised to help them develop a harbor that could accommodate more ships and safely moor them overnight without any crew. We also said we would give them safe passage through Roman water and tax-free access to all Roman markets. In exchange, they must bend their knees, swear allegiance to the emperor, and pay taxes.*

*But when we tell them everyone must pay taxes, they validate our evidence that they are not civilized. I cannot understand why giving a tenth of all they make to Rome is so challenging for them. They get to keep nine-tenths.*

*Once we passed through the straights, we found the opposite of hospitality in Gadir. As we approached the first small harbor, the cavemen who lived there began shooting at us with catapults and arrows. Our watercraft was designed for this resistance and we landed on shore without casualties. However, when we stepped onto the land, the people came at us like madmen. Our translator stood on a portable platform so that he could speak and all could hear him. We covered him in our best armor while our centurion told him what to say.*

*'Greetings, people of this land. We come with messages from the emperor and wish to talk to you about your inclusion into our great empire.' Our translator listened to their leader speak and he translated back for us, telling us that these people thought we were of the devil. Their leader told his men to slit our throats and that they should fight until no one was left standing.*

*After hearing these words, our centurion shook his head in disgust and told us to beat them to a pulp. Their lack of quality armor or weapons made the work relatively easy. After each death, our centurion would re-engage their leader, asking him if he was ready to submit. After a few iterations of this kill-and-talk affair, our centurion decided to change tactics.*

*We could hear a few dogs barking in the distance. Looking up, we could see their small village situated inside the woods. Women and children gathered at the village's edge and they watched their men try to defend them from afar. Many were crying and the mothers held their children as they watched us overpower them. I suspect that is what made all the dogs bark.*

*At one point, their leader yelled, 'Nothing you do to my men will make us stop fighting you!' I remember his men raising their weapons and shouting some barbaric war cry. Once we heard that, our centurion gave me and my squad new directions. He sent me into the village and told me to bring back a pregnant woman. Without thinking, I took nine men and flanked the village from the north, entering on a trail through the nearby path we found. We carefully hid ourselves using the buildings and identified two pregnant women. Once we did, I split my men into two groups and we each quickly captured these women and carried them back to the boat. Each woman was gagged and our centurion engaged the soldiers himself to draw their attention away from the men returning with the two captured women.*

*His plan worked perfectly. He told me to attach each woman to the front of the boat so they could not leave us or the water. We placed a wall of soldiers in front of them as they stood in waist-deep water so these tribal men could see their women. We also cut off all their clothes so everyone could see they were pregnant.*

*Once they saw their women bound to the boat, our centurion spoke to their men through the translator.*

*'As you have said, there is nothing I can do to your men to make you stop fighting us and bend the knee. However, there is something I can do to your women,' he said.*

*I can remember what he told me. In fact, I will never forget the words he used.*

*'Cornelius! Cut between that animal's vagina and her belly button with your hunting knife, cut out that half-baby, and hand it to me, boy.'*

*I was a disciplined warrior; these cavemen had just attacked and attempted to kill some of my brothers. What could I do?*

*'Cornelius! Perform the Caesarian section!' said our leader in a much louder voice.*

*I sheathed my sword and took out my hunting knife, wiping it clean using seawater and a cloth. The woman must have known what was about to happen as she began to scream through her gag. I did as my centurion instructed. However, I made a mistake. I looked her in the eye after I started the cut, and I saw her agony. She was screaming in her rage and repeating something in her native language that I could not understand. Once I made the final cut, the Centurion spoke to me again.*

*"You must cut deeper to cut through the walls of the womb. It is a thick muscle. Move aside! Let me have your knife and I will show you!"*

*I was humiliated. I cannot believe I could not perform a simple half-cubit cut. Within two breaths, I watched the centurion finish what I could not. He reached inside of her as she entered shock, and he pulled out the grey mass of the unborn child from the mother. Then he walked towards an opening in the line of soldiers. He held the unborn child high enough so all the men of Gadir could see. Then he killed it.*

*Through the translator, he spoke to the men.*

*"I tell you this again, take a knee," and he waited.*

*Some of the barbarians entered into fits of rage and attempted to run at the centurion; however, our two best archers were ready, putting an arrow in each person's gut before taking ten steps. Their leader failed to respond to our centurion. After another brief pause, our leader spoke to me.*

*"Cornelius, the other unborn child, please," he said.*

*I was not about to feel shame a second time in a day. Without hesitating, I quickly took to the task of taking the next woman's unborn child. I promptly brought it to our leader to make up for my previous mistake.*

*"Well done, boy. You are a quick learner," he said. I yearned for affirmation from him and wanted to show my loyalty.*

*"Sir, let me, " I asked.*

*"Of course," he said. As our Roman training had taught us, he and I stepped closer to Gadir's leader.*

*"Bend the knee," he said.*

*Their leader shook his head in disagreement. We had all been taught that we must be persistent and unyielding. Our goal was very specific, and our tactics had proven successful for many generations. I knew that I must have faith in Rome's methods if*

*I wished to grow in military ranks. The next step made perfect sense to me. After all, it was only a half-human.*

*I stuck the child with my knife and it died. This unborn was much older than the first, and its eyes were open. I paused to look and saw that it had brown eyes, a full head of hair, and an open mouth. It wore a disgustingly grey skin color, yet I could see it was a human female child.*

*However, when I struck it, it felt like a piece of my human foundation cracked and I was no longer the civilized man. In fact, I felt like the barbarians in front of me. I felt rage. I felt shame. I hated them and I hated me.*

*In retrospect, I see that this dead child and its sliced-open mother were innocent of any crime. It was being forced to pay for the sins of its leader. The unborn had done nothing wrong, but it would not receive a chance to live. Indeed, my military advancement was contingent on my effectiveness in performing this task, but I could not see myself repeating this action. My blade passed through its body like lard. This act was nearly effortless on my body, but my soul was broken.*

*'Don't look at the baby or me. Look at their leader like you are looking at the emperor,' my centurion ordered.*

*I turned and faced the leader, holding my blade in my right hand. I wiped it clean with some of the woman's clothing that was now floating on the shores of the Mediterranean. I remembered my teachings. Rome ruled with predictable displays of power and a ruthless commitment to forced submission. Rome ruled the world by the discipline of the men who fought on the front line, and I was proud to be one of those men. It remained my goal to be one of the leaders of this great force. Carthage was the majesty many years before, and Rome was the upstart. Now, Rome is in the world's majesty, and I was one of its representatives.*

*I had memorized the translator's words and I spoke them with a calm yet stern voice.*

*'Take the knee,' I repeated. My centurion looked at me, smiling, and said I had used the same tone and words as the translator.*

*With that, their leader dropped his makeshift sword and took the knee, sobbing uncontrollably. Through the translator, every man in the village took a knee and swore allegiance to Rome. They all agreed to pay taxes in exchange for our protection and services that unite the empire. Once the last man had completed his oath, the centurion spoke to the newest member of the Roman Empire.*

*'You now have access to all that is Rome. You will have access to our transportation, protection, and a voice in our republic in Rome. You shall elect and send two men and their escorts to the city for training in the next moon cycle. Welcome to freedom and power that you cannot understand.'"*

Caleb was sobbing before he finished the last paragraph. He spoke out loud despite the fact that no one nearby could hear him.

"What the hell kind of man were you? I trusted you!" He looked up and shook his head as he gazed over the Mediterranean. With that pause, Caleb vomited as he pondered what he had just read. Then he fell to his knees and began sobbing deeply. He covered his mouth as he didn't need for his wife to hear. She might come up and ask him what was wrong, and she could not be allowed to see what was in this document. For her sake, he needed to keep the contents of this scroll to himself. Perhaps one day, he could show it to his lieutenants, but that was not this day.

"I will never do this sort of thing!" he swore under his whispering breath. One of the servants who had just inherited great wealth heard him and quietly came up the stairs. Without thinking, Caleb turned to him and erupted in anger. He shook the scroll with his hand as he expressed his rage.

"I hate Rome. I hate what this job does to us. I hate what it has done to my family. I hate Cornelius!" The servant forced himself to smile and held back his desire to laugh. He was wise, and he knew that the person before him was not the centurion of Caesarea; it was a wounded young man looking for an outlet to express his pain at whatever he read in that ancient scroll. The servant had seen Cornelius in this state before and he had watched Caleb and his wife navigate the impact of Rome on the heart of its leaders.

"Caleb, come here," he said. He opened his arms, walked up, and hugged him as hard as he could. Caleb broke down and wept deeply, allowing the servant to comfort him. Finally, he pushed Caleb away, looked up at the hulk of a man, and spoke to him. He hoped he was speaking into his heart and could continue the message that Cornelius was trying to teach.

"Cornelius did not find answers to the question about the presence of great evil in this world, either," said the servant. Caleb knew that the servant understood his pain and he thanked him for being there. The servant held Caleb until he stopped crying and he looked him in the eye, almost as if he were Cornelius.

"Centurion, Cornelius loved you deeply. You were his pride and joy. I don't know what you just read, but it was meant to help you grow in your job and in your faith. He had good reason not to share that with you until he had passed away. Cornelius was thoughtful and wise in his instruction. Whatever it was that hurt you, it was not meant to be permanent. Will you be OK?"

"Not today. My faith is wounded. I am wounded. I am disgusted with Cornelius, and I want to take my son for a walk," Caleb said. He rolled the scroll back up and knew he needed to hide its contents from the girls. He handed it to the servant and told him to put it back in the basement when no one was watching.

"We are praying for you, Centurion," the servant said as he left.

He entered the kitchen, walking briskly. Yael could tell he had been crying, but he didn't want to talk to his wife. Instead, he was focused on finding Mishi. The little boy was sound asleep and Caleb gently picked him up, telling his wife that he needed to go for a walk. The solace on Caleb's face seemed to melt like ice in the summer once he picked up his little boy. Yael could see the first aid of an innocent child operating in the hands of a hurting father, and she smiled.

"Caleb, I love you," she said.

"I love you, too," said Eliza.

"I know," he said, and they could see that he was crying again.

Caleb took Mishi out of earshot, sat down on one of the family benches, and let his little boy rest in his lap, his head off to one side as he slept. Caleb took a deep breath and spoke to the boy the way that he often did.

"My son, I hope you don't make the mistakes that my uncle made. I hope I don't, either. This Caesarean cutting open of women is beyond evil." He sobbed uncontrollably, shaking as if he were freezing.

"And the city I serve in is named after it!" his crying intensified. He wanted to throw up again. This moment felt worse than witnessing a crucifixion.

"Son, I am broken and I don't know what to do. Oh, Mishi, I pray for you. I can't do this." He paused to let his tears fall for a moment. Then he composed himself and wiped the tears from his eyes. He had to trust his uncle's reason for giving him this scroll, even though he did not know what they were.

"I know Uncle Cornelius could not tell me this story while he was alive, but at least he gave it to me in death. I hope I do not have to tell you about it, but I fear I might. I want to burn this scroll. I bet your great uncle knew that. That is why he kept it. God! I hate that I needed to know that! Damn it!" Caleb spoke the Lord's name at high volume, and it startled his son, but Caleb rocked him back to sleep.

"That is why I am going to keep it. I have to keep it. One day, you will be a great leader, and you will marry a powerful woman. You will have children of your own and there will be evils from my times that I will hide from you. You may need the contents of this scroll to guide you. I hate saying that, but it will be great guidance for you one day, just as it has been for me." Caleb whimpered for a moment, trying to compose himself.

"Pray for your father, my son. Pray that he does not repeat what his uncle did. Pray that he follows the lessons of the cross instead of putting people on them. I don't know how Uncle Cornelius did it. Just pray for your father, my son. Now, let's get you back in the bed," Caleb said.

Of all the things Cornelius had taught him, little boys like Mishi are the best medicine for the evil in the world. Little boys know how to receive love and listen like no one else.

And in that moment of great melancholy, Caleb discovered that he had been Cornelius' little boy.

# Chapter 9:
# To Yael: Of Rape

It was the start of a new day. Caleb held her tightly all night and his hands gently explored every part of her in the early hours of the morning. She knew he needed to connect with her, and she allowed herself to feel the joy he intended for her. He fell asleep afterward and he snored as his body craved rest after the trauma he felt reading the scrolls of Cornelius. She kissed him gently, got up, and let him continue to rest. He sacrificed everything for her and this was the least she could do.

Some of the servants greeted her in the kitchen and they acted as if nothing had changed. They were now wealthy beyond measure, yet nothing about their behavior was different. They cut vegetables, prepared tea, swept the floors, kneaded fresh bread, and soaked the beans. All of yesterday's clothing was already washed and drying outside on the line. They had plans to put more broccoli and spinach seeds in the ground this afternoon and harvest oranges to take to the markets and sell. Caleb had told her to expect that they would continue with life as normal and she now believed him.

"You girls are wonderful. Thank you for your service to this family." Yael said. They brushed off her comments and poured Yael a cup of hot tea made with fresh camel milk.

"Some tea?" the older servant asked.

"Of course! And join me!" she said. Her happiness was obvious and she felt gregarious around her staff. She sat down, took her child from her maid, and began nursing it.

"We have already prayed that you and master have more children," said her maid as gracefully as she could. All the women looked at Yael and laughed. They knew that she and Caleb had made love during the night. Yael did not know how they knew, as Caleb kept quiet when he knew that others might hear them, but somehow, these women always knew.

"The master adores you. You must feel blessed," said her maid as she saw Yael blush.

The servants told her that Val was still asleep, and some of them had slept with her. Val knew that her husband was no longer suffering and she took this as a chance to rest.

"Today is the day, ladies!" she announced. They all knew that this was her day to prove to her sister that she had learned to read and write the Greek language. When she met Eliza a few years earlier in the Roman Coliseum, she could barely speak Greek. During the last few months, Cornelius took her to the basement during his quiet times, and she read out loud to him until she got everything right. She wrote it down, and she learned what each word meant and how it was used. His strategy was abrasive, but she had watched him mentor Caleb and knew what to expect. She also knew he was intelligent and knew how to teach. And he loved her and wanted what was best.

"You are a dumb farmer girl. Read that again! You sound like a drunk beggar with leprosy. Make it sound like you are a rich Roman this time. That is what you are with all the jewelry you wear on your neck and hands." She would smile at him once he called her down like that, and she would try again. Eventually, she would get it right, and he would let her know how proud he was.

Cornelius' strategy was simple. He would get her to say the same line repeatedly until her pronunciation was nearly identical to his. He would show her a section of the text, then cover it up, telling her to write down what she had just seen, and he would have her read it to him until she could start to see the patterns of transcription and scribing. Finally, he would bring back papers from his office in Caesarea and have her read them. Eventually, she learned to read advertisements from merchants and new decrees signed by and, in some cases, written by her husband. Caleb and Cornelius were proud of her and encouraged her every chance they got.

Best of all, she always looked forward to Cornelius' hugs. He was a massive man, nearly the same size as her husband, but he was always gentle with her and quick to tell her how much he loved her. His beard was as white as snow and scraggly. He called it his white bird's nest, and when she put her head on his chest, she could feel it against the side of her face. She loved how it felt and she knew that one day, Caleb would have the same white beard. She hoped that Caleb would have Cornelius' countenance when he was older and not be uptight about getting everything right.

"Thank you for taking care of my husband," she would always tell him during their study times. She had watched him mentor Caleb from afar many times over the years, and her husband had become a very loving man. Her treated her like a princess; all he wanted in exchange was respect and her to enjoy sex as much as he did. Val taught her that part, but Cornelius' times with Caleb would always be her fondest memory of him.

"Boy, that is your woman in the kitchen. You don't have to share her with Caesar. She is all yours now. Treat her like it, you dumb ass!" he would say. Caleb would stand stoically in front of the old man when he talked to him like this, as she sometimes watched Cornelius dress him down as if he were a slave. She did not tell Caleb, but she knew that submitting to his authority was making him a better man.

Yael didn't know how often Cornelius tore down her husband's authority like that, but she knew when it had happened, as he would enter the kitchen, look at her, and act as if he had seen a ghost. Val told her she needed to act surprised when he arrived and did not let on that she knew he was being reprimanded. Val told her to keep quiet and let her husband do the hard work of expressing himself. She promised he would get better as he aged and she just needed patience. She told her it was worth the wait.

"Yael, I love you. I don't want to do life without you," he learned to say. She knew he meant it. That meant he was grateful to have her in his life. It also meant he submitted the stewardship of his home and his wealth to her. The way he treated her in court was no different than the way she treated him when they were in the kitchen. Every kiss in the kitchen and every "I love you" were her prompts to know that Cornelius had just broken him down and built him back up again.

Yael remembered the last time Cornelius had his wits about him and could speak to Caleb. Cornelius had Caleb sit on the rooftop in front of him on the morning of Shabbat. Yael was at the bottom of the stairs with Eliza, quietly listening to the two of them like two schoolgirls.

"Boy, how much time does it take to tell her you missed her when you were away from here? Huh? Will you fall over dead with hunger if you tell her she is the light of your life before you ask what is for dinner?" Caleb remained speechless as he listened but after a few moments, Cornelius would go back at him.

"You are as dumb as a rock in the Jordan River. Don't you see who she is? She is more important than your job or me, for that matter. When you get home, empty your heart to her, even if you are done in a single breath. Just do it, and then worry about what you need to do. She will act like she can wait, but in her heart, your attention is all she wants. Don't be an idiot. That is my job," he would say.

Caleb would sometimes ask about what life is like after being married for 20 or 30 years. Yael liked listening to Caleb and Cornelius interact, as it would prompt her to ask Val the same question later.

"One day, your beautiful young bride will look just like Val, covered in wrinkles and moving like a turtle on a sandy beach. If you do what I am telling you, you will love her more, and she will love you more than you do after you have had sex with her. And she will still be beautiful. Call it magic or something. I don't know; it just works." He suspected he told Caleb that more than once, but she remembers that one time the most.

Caleb encouraged her time learning from Cornelius. Yael was more confident when she would have a longer session with Cornelius.

"Your language skills are improving!" he would tell his wife. He would speak to her in Aramaic occasionally and she answered him in Ebreet. She could now understand the ancient language of the people who used to live in this area during the great exile. She would practice her Greek with him, and when they would go to court together, she would speak only Greek.

Eliza though had no idea that Yael was becoming a language scholar. She was spending most of her time at the House of Healing with Dor. Now, Yael felt confident and ready to read out loud to her already-scholarly sister. This morning was the big chance to show her what she had learned. Eliza had just come down to join them and she sat next to her sister as the servants gave her a cup of tea.

"Here, Eliza, burp Mishi. I am going to read to you." After her sister had her baby, she looked up at her, took a deep breath, and started her tale.

"Eliza, I am sure no woman has heard the contents of this scroll other than me. You don't know this, but uncle taught me how to read and write with scrolls that held stories like this one."

"Really? I can't wait!" said Eliza.

Eliza's heart raced. She knew this was what her sister was talking about in the basement.

"The content is abrasive, but you and I have already talked about these things in our lives."

"OK," said Eliza, with a sense of hesitation. Yael leaned forward and kissed her sister on the cheek. Eliza's nervousness was obvious as difficult conversations about injustice were unnatural for her. She looked for something to say or do to address her fidgetiness, and she just started burping Mishi as her sister prepared to read to her for the first time. All she knew was that her heart was charged for too many reasons to consider. It was a longer scroll, and she needed space to unroll all of it before she started.

"I can already tell that this story will upset me," said Eliza.

"It will. I know you. He has talked to me about it many times, as this is a temptation that Caleb will face. You and I should talk about it, too," Yael said. With that, she began reading her uncle's story. Eliza was impressed that her pronunciation was perfect.

> *"This afternoon, we completed our capture of a village in East Gall. Although these people are not civilized, there are some things that they possess that are valuable. Part of the benefit of overseas assignments is the permission we have to take what we*

*want from the bounty as part of our victory right; the poor bastards in the army who sleep in their beds back home each night get no bonuses, nor do they get to pillage. Indeed, it is in the aftermath of winning a battle that we can genuinely earn our fair compensation.*

*However, today's conquest in this small, godless village unsettled me. None of the other men in our squad appeared as perplexed by what happened as I was. I am unsure if I would share this story out loud, but I need to write it down to begin sorting out what I think happened."*

"So, this writing is something like 50 years old, isn't it?" Eliza asked. Yael nodded in agreement. "I think so, but I never asked him. In fact, he never talked about how old this is. Each time we read it, he would kiss me and love me like I was the last person in the world." Yael said.

"Please, keep going," said Eliza, feeling a bit more ready to receive the words.

*"To begin, I remain disturbed by a pattern among these Aboriginals in Gall. When we arrive, we tell them that we represent Rome and have taken possession of these lands. We tell them they can continue to go about their business affairs and cultural rituals as they wish. However, they must pay tribute to Rome each year. In exchange, Rome would provide them with expansive access to markets beyond their dreams for their goods. We will give them public road systems and maintain them. We will give them military protection from invaders. This is certainly better than anything offered to them by Carthage or the other half-human leaders in this part of the world.*

*Yet, today, as is nearly always the case, this village's leader did not accept our proposal. Stupid fools! Their stupidity and stubbornness took a familiar form. They chose to fight us with inferior weapons and almost no combat training. This unintelligent act explains why all of us consider them to be uncivilized. Why are they not choosing the well-being of their families over the false value of freedom? They don't know how to make iron weapons and tools in this part of the world. No wonder they are so ignorant of the world's affairs. I wonder why these savages think they can defeat us.*

*Today's resulting loss of life was another waste of our time. Now, most of the strong men of this tribe lay in puddles of their blood, and most of the families of what is left of this village have no male leader. Considering how poor they already are, I don't see how they will survive without first becoming someone else's property. For my share, I am taking three women and one boy as my property, and I hope to sell them once we reach the coast. That is the most important part of my story."*

"Uncle Cornelius took women as slaves?" Eliza asked. Not since the time of the prophets had anyone from the twelve tribes done this. Yael didn't respond other than to look up, smile, and continue reading.

*"Moments after this morning's fighting ended, we soldiers surveyed the village grounds and cleaned off our weapons to prevent rusting. Most of the men who fought us had stopped breathing already. Those who were wounded we finished off with spears as quickly as possible, for we all know that listening to dying men, even these half-men, can create haunting memories in the night. Once we finished that*

*task, I moved my men into the village's center to look for bounty. The village was smaller than we first thought; there was one village warehouse, and most of the contents were grain, oil, and dried meat. Indeed, none of their garbage food was worth risking our lives for, and we felt indignant about finding some reward to pay us for the risk we just took. A few men agreed to take the village ale as their share of the bounty, and a few of us took the villagers themselves as our share of the prize.*

*Many of the women whose homes we burned were huddled against a dais to some false god. Most held their children close to them and both women and children smelled as if they had defecated on themselves. I was saddened to think how stupid and scared these half-apes were. They could all have kept their families had their men submitted. We could have funded a school for some young boys and perhaps helped them build a road supporting larger carts and carriages. Now, they have nothing but a life of slavery ahead of them. They are fools.*

*However, the stench of the women did not defer my friend Galba's lust for flesh. He and I are big men, and as we walked through the village, these half-women viewed us as some god. We stood more than a head taller than any of the men and nearly two heads taller than all the women. I wondered what these women saw as they stared at our armor and gladius; it must have felt like hades had been opened and poured out among them.*

*Galba had already made it clear it was his turn to pick first among the women. There were perhaps twenty to choose between and Galba talked to several other men about which one he might enjoy the most. None of these women understood our lan-*

*guage, and they trembled and looked down as Galba surveyed their faces and bodies.*

*He picked the best one with blonde hair and he decided that he would have her. She had one young child clinging to her leg. He turned to me and spoke,*

*"Cornelius, how do you say in their language, 'I am having you, now!'"*

*"Most veletek vagyok," I said. After placing his right hand on her son's arm, he looked at her and spoke those words to her.*

*She screamed and all of us laughed. He pulled the child from her and cast the boy towards me. When the boy stopped rolling at my feet, I wrapped my arm over his chest and held him next to me so he could not move.*

*"Corn, hold that boy while I take my fair portion of the bounty!" he said, wearing a huge smile.*

*Galba proceeded to rape the woman. I know these half-people deserved to be raped for the actions of their men. That was apparent; they defied the emperor's demands and were lucky we did not kill them all. After all, I told their men when we first entered their village that they would be punished if they resisted us. It seemed fair that this woman paid the price for her husband's lack of submission.*

*Yet, something didn't seem OK at that moment. I could not look on as all the other men cheered for Galba to finish in style. I wondered what it was that I found so wrong that prevented me from finding pleasure in this. I certainly have before!*

*I lifted the crying boy and took him around the corner of the nearest house. He kept saying, 'Mommy, mommy,' between his sobbing and tears.*

*Once we rounded the corner, I sat him down and removed my gauntlets and helmet so he could see me. He saw the cut on my eye from when I was younger and the grime and sweat on my face that came with walking days and nights. I squatted next to him so that he could look me in the eyes. I kept a clean cloth inside my belt pouch and wiped the tears from his eyes.*

*'My friend will release your mother very soon,' I said. Their language was simple and I had already learned how to use the basics. He nodded as if he understood me. Certainly, he did nothing wrong and I decided he needed to be removed from this event. I am glad I could do that for him.*

*The boy continued a low-level crying and my unsettled feelings grew. I picked him up and held him like my father would hold my little brother, resting his head on his shoulder while my father rubbed his head. Once the cheers ended and I knew Galba was done, I took the boy around the corner to his mother. When I walked around the edge of the building, I saw a different man in our unit telling Galba that he would do the boy's mother next.*

*At that point, something happened inside of me, and I snapped. I set the boy down next to his mother and unsheathed my gladius. I spoke to that man, telling him this woman had enough and needed her strength to care for her child. I threatened to strike anyone who attempted to rape her again. For my part, though, it wasn't until later that I discovered that I had unsheathed my weapon. In fact, it was Galba that told me. It must have been my protective instinct.*

*I could not control my rage. I stepped between the next soldier and the woman and looked her in the eye. She closed her eyes as soon as we made contact, but she did not look away, somehow seeing that I was intervening for her and the boy. The two of them clung to each other and neither of them cried now. It was as if they could see that I was their pro-tector. One of the men told me that my knuckles were turning white from my grip on my blade. No one spoke to me after that and we quickly packed up what each of us claimed and left the village.*

*We are now camped a quarter day south of the village and are less than two days from the coast. I intend to sell the two other women I kept from the spoils when we arrive. However, I have decided to let the raped woman and her son go free. As always, they walked behind me as if they were my possessions now.*

*As we traversed lightly traveled roads on our way toward the coast, I thought about the sadness of their condition. Something in me spoke to me and commanded me to speak out loud words I heard as a boy. I believe I now know what they meant. I said,*

*Defend those who cannot help themselves. Speak up for the poor and helpless and see that they get justice.*

*Some men asked me what kind of justice they would get as I spoke those words repeatedly, but I couldn't answer them. As expected, they laughed and asked if I had too much ale. I couldn't laugh with them as I usually do, as I could see that the raped woman was traumatized. However, she kept her focus on her son, knowing she needed to be there for him, no matter how traumatized she was. I don't know if that makes her more human or more like an instinctual animal.*

*Nothing about these last two days seemed right. I was embarrassed by what Galba did to her. Yet if I pull away all the layers of stigma, I must ask the question, 'How many times have I done the same thing?'"*

Yael looked up at Eliza, knowing Eliza was about to say something.

"I don't know what to say. My mind cannot comprehend this. Uncle Cornelius was a rapist?" Eliza rhetorically said. Eliza looked like she was ready to vomit. Yael calmly responded to her.

"He told me that is what everyone did back then. It wasn't considered bad and no one told him not to," Yael said.

"Wait. That scroll is what he used to teach you how to read and write Greek?" Eliza asked. Yael nodded yes.

"My Lord, Yael! This is awful! There were so many better choices. Are you OK?" Eliza asked.

"Eliza, you know I have been repeatedly raped. You and I shared a room where Benji helped me start healing. I think uncle knew both of us could handle this." Eliza shook her head in disbelief, tears flowing from her eyes in buckets. She looked down to see that Mishi had fallen asleep to the sound of his mother's voice.

"Oh, God! I can see why Caleb comes home and takes this little boy for a walk. I don't know what I would do if I were not holding him right now," Eliza said.

"Let me finish," Yael said. She continued reading the last part of the letter.

> *"Yet in these quiet moments of thought, I replayed the narrative. Something was working inside of me in ways that I could not explain. My father always told me that I could not fix the past, but I could perhaps change the future.*
>
> *The morning we reached the coast, I gave the woman enough coin to support her and the boy for a month. Hopefully, she can find work at the harbor and provide for the boy. If not, she will become another prostitute. I have done all that I can now.*
>
> *On a side note, I got two barrels of ale for the other women I kept. Perhaps I can drink away these feelings that are overwhelming me. During the transaction, I avoided eye contact with these women*

*as they pleaded with me for coins like I had given the raped woman and her child. They said I was being unfair. The truth is they were right. I felt guilty despite not doing anything wrong. At least I saved one of them. I decided then and there that these women needed to pay the price for their husband's disobedience. Someone had to.*

*That moment with the two other half-women gave me a moment to ponder. I wondered how my life might be different if I was held responsible for my father's transgressions. Galba's children will certainly not know of this transgression, as he will not speak to them of it.*

*I am wondering now what I should do with my life. I no longer like working on the frontier and the extra salary that comes with the risk. I don't want to rape and pillage anymore. There is something wrong when this is the goal in life. But I don't know what it is.*

*May the gods bless the half-human souls of these Aboriginals and take away this sick feeling that is now resident in me".*

Yael looked up as soon as she finished. She expected to hear her sister congratulate her on her proficiency in Greek. Instead, she found that she needed to take her baby back from her as she had been quietly sobbing throughout the last part of the reading. Mishi had come out from his nap and Yael immediately started nursing him again while Eliza composed herself. Eliza gestured for one of the servants to prepare another pot of tea for the two of them. When Eliza finally could speak, she was at a loss as to where to start.

"How could he use that to teach you?" she rhetorically asked. Yael smiled. She had already asked him that question. Yael waited another moment before responding to let her sister's heart catch up.

"Because I told him and Val everything that happened to me when I was a slave in Rome. They knew I would empathize with these characters."

Eliza looked at her with near rage as she spoke.

"I know that! That is why I am so upset right now!" Mishi began to cry as Eliza screamed. She apologized and let Yael regulate the baby.

"Why did he think that reopening that wound with you or with me would be a good idea?" she asked. Eliza shifted her body so she could sit next to her sister.

"I did ask him that. He said that you and I are going to make sure that this will ensure that my children and your children are not rapists!" she said. Eliza liked that answer. It made her think and she compared what she was hearing from Yael with what Dor had been teaching her. Exposure to older trauma, a little at a bit, is part of healing. Cornelius' idea to use this story to teach her began to make some sense.

"Auntie asked me many questions about my time in the palace. Uncle was quiet for days after I shared my story with them. I saw the look on his face as she and I talked. I saw that it wounded him for me to recant my story as much as the truth of this one is wounding you now. But it is the truth." Eliza nodded for a moment, realizing that her sister had thought about this more than she had.

"Remember how good it felt when we told each other about our experiences with rape on the boat ride home from Rome? I think he needed to share that story with you and me, and he felt we could handle it." There was a long pause as the two women sat with each other and drank tea.

"Caleb said that uncle spoke to him about my rape one morning, but he did not mention it after that. After I told uncle about my raping, he has made a habit of telling me that he loves me every day. Eliza, I am telling you the truth. He told me every single day," said Yael. Eliza wiped away some more tears before Yael continued.

"After he heard my story, he used to kiss and hold me like I was the most precious person in his life. Val always smiled and cried when she watched him pour his love into me. There is more story there than we will be allowed to hear, sister. I think this letter is part of his repentance for participating. Perhaps this is part of his love for me."

The two girls looked at each other and nodded. Her conclusions were right. After some light conversation, Yael stepped into her flowering role as a leader and spoke to Eliza. She was the subject matter expert on this topic.

"Eliza, I have learned that centurions are passionate. They are powerful and desperate for real connection. Yet they are as brittle as glass dropped on a rock. I am glad that I am loved by two of them. Both of them would die for me. And they would die for you, too." The two of them shared some small talk and tales of what Caleb did when he was younger before Yael brought the conversation back.

"I have had a lot of time to reflect on what Uncle Cornelius was trying to teach me. I think he was trying to do right by me these last months because he didn't do right by others." After saying that, Yael stared at the ground in front of her.

Eliza nodded in agreement.

"And I think Val has stories we will never know about, too," said Yael.

"Why else would he give you this story?" Eliza tried to articulate the obvious. These men loved Yael and Eliza without conditions. They stared at the feeding baby as they attempted to avoid the discomfort they felt, knowing how much each of these men was hurting.

"Certainly, he knows this story impacts our critique of him," Eliza said.

"Sister, I asked him about this when he taught me to read. He didn't try to defend himself or say something positive about Val. You know what he said?"

She paused before answering.

"The desire of the flesh is the way of men. It is beautiful when used for good, like the making of this beautiful boy or when I comfort Caleb as he returns from a day of struggle and unspoken hurt. However, Sheol also uses it for perverse acts to fulfill desires meant to be fulfilled in the marriage bed. Yahweh has always guided us against this act, yet men still do it. After all, it is mentioned twice in Moses's commandments and throughout the Torah."

She paused for a moment before Eliza spoke.

"Sister, you should be a Torah teacher. I could not have said that any better," said Eliza. Yael laughed and blushed. Yael greatly desired Eliza's affirmation and her compliment meant the world to her. She felt confident about continuing to share what she had learned.

"Nearly all God-fearing male leaders struggled with this desire. David did. Solomon did. Now I know that our uncle did, too," Yael finished.

Eliza nodded her head as she knew what Yael was referencing from the scrolls of the prophets. Her experience in Rome validated that men would look at her body with lust in their eyes when she wore provocative clothing. Of course, she could not forget the time she was held down by three men wanting to rape her.

"You are wise enough for two women, Yael," Eliza said, further enriching Yael's soul. The two of them stared at each other and forced a smile. They sat in silence for a few moments until the baby finished nursing and fell asleep. Yael handed the baby back to Eliza and stood up to get some more firewood for the kitchen fire. As she stirred the coals and added new fuel, she gave Eliza some more of Cornelius' teachings.

"Uncle warned me that the accidental pursuit of the flesh will be a problem for Caleb as he progresses through the military ranks and spends time in Rome. Uncle also told me that Caleb has the power to say yes or no to this desire, but unfortunately, it will have nothing to do with me or how I treat him. Uncle told me that he remembered the walk to the coast with that woman and her son each time the desire to sleep with another woman came upon him, and it was enough to carry him through his struggles. However, when loved ones fall victim to the desires of the flesh, families can fall."

"Eliza, one day you will have a husband and children, too. Cornelius knew that. That is why he told me to read it to you," Yael said. Eliza looked up at the ceiling and finished her tea.

"What are you going to do with that lesson?" Eliza asked.

"Auntie Val told me that there is exactly one tool in my arsenal to combat this desire. It is prayer. Each day, therefore, I pray for Caleb to find that I am enough and that he does not seek to fill the voids in his life away from me."

Eliza stared at her sister. She knew that Yael had learned more than just Greek from Uncle Cornelius. He had also been teaching her the Talmud of the Rabbis of old, and she had developed the wisdom of a woman three times her age.

"That, and to look pretty for him."

"Well, that isn't hard for you! Caleb had eyes for you the moment the two of you first spoke when he was embarrassed to clean up the food he dropped," Eliza said. They laughed as they recalled that magical moment in the boxes within the Coliseum.

"And make sure he has tasty food. Auntie reminded me that Esau sold his birthright for a bowl of stew. Had he not done that, we all would be saying, 'the God of Abraham, Isaac, and Esau' instead."

Their deep laughter eventually ceased and Caleb returned from his rooftop reading. He had a look on his face that they knew too well. Despite the size of his physique and the power of his blade and bow, they could sense that he had just been wounded. He reached out for his son, not interested in revealing what was happening inside of him. He took Mishi and turned to leave.

"I will be right back. And don't ask me where we are going. I don't know." Caleb said.

"Caleb, we love you," said Eliza, but he did not show any signs that he had heard her.

"Don't worry. He heard you," said Yael.

"I know. I, too, have had two centurions in my life," said Eliza, smiling.

# Chapter 10:
# Of reconciliation of sin

The two sisters tried many things to get Caleb to talk after he came back from his time with Mishi. He was still shaking and couldn't speak without sobbing. They asked him what was wrong, why he was crying, and what the scroll's contents might have been. Caleb used to think this aggressive inquiry was a form of ganging up against him, but he has learned otherwise. Aunt Val told him in no uncertain words that it was his job to be gentle with these two women, that he needed to make peace, and that no matter what he thought was happening, they meant well. God designed women to be helpers, even though they do not appear to be that way as they use words.

He knew he could trust them with the most intimate part of his being, but he couldn't make peace with the reality that he couldn't trust them with the truth. They couldn't handle this content. He knew he would feel better if he told them, but they would not be better.

Perhaps he couldn't speak to them but he could love them. He opened his empty arm and they came to him and embraced him. He handed Mishi back to his wife so that he could hug Yael and Eliza simultaneously. He kissed each of them. Both of them still had their hair down from the previous night and he caressed their heads the way they liked him to.

"Girls, you know I love you, but what I just read, I cannot share with you. Not ever. Uncle experienced a burden uniquely known to men on the frontier and he knew this was a burden that could not be shared. Certainly, Cornelius could not share it with auntie. This is my burden to bear. Please try to understand."

They looked him in the eye and processed his words. He was pleading with them as politely as he could. But both girls had learned from Val, which is one of the most important messages about life as a wife and cousin when your husband is powerful and in charge.

"Every centurion was a young boy at one time, seeking affirmation and affection from the ones he loved. A fancy title, a powerful body, armor, jewelry, wealth, and weapons do not completely cover what is underneath. Part of him shall always remain a little boy. Remember that: speak to that little boy with love, and he will bind to you all his days."

"Caleb, you are a great protector. I know you will do the right thing to keep us safe. I am sorry that you are hurting," said Eliza. Caleb nodded in acknowledgment and kissed Eliza. Yael knew her job was to reinforce and not present something new when nothing new was necessary. Caleb dealt with new problems every day. She needed to separate and represent his stable rock.

"You are the father of our child, and I am dependent on you for my well-being. Eliza said everything on behalf of both of us," his wife said.

"Thank you," he said.

"I always love it when you hold me like this, cousin," Eliza said, putting her ear against his chest and closing her eyes. Caleb kissed her again on the top of her head and massaged her beautiful dark hair just as he did when they were growing up. He felt that he could speak a few words now.

"I know that uncle meant for the lesson in that scroll to cut through the hardness of my core being, but I wasn't ready for it on the day after we buried him. I am sure that he knew it would make an impact. I hate it, but I must trust that he knew what was best." Everyone stared at the fire, each deep in independent thought. Yael broke the silence.

"How about we reheat some of the food from the banquet, along with some of auntie's wine in the cistern? We have a lot of leftover wine, perhaps enough for a year."

She looked at her sister and winked.

"Then I know what you two are going to do," said Eliza. Caleb blushed, as he always did when either of them mentioned sex. Caleb refused to acknowledge that what Yael had just offered him made her the most beautiful woman who had ever lived. But she knew.

"Perhaps we can drink a cup or two," said Caleb.

In the same way that Caleb was doing his part to protect them from evil, Yael was doing her part to keep her husband from sin.

# Chapter 11:
# To Eliza, the first letter to Titus.

The following day, Eliza woke and prepared tea and bread for everyone, as Yael had given all the servants the day off to spend some of their inheritance. As soon as the ceremonial meal at first light was over, Eliza and her mother prepared for a morning together.

"You girls have fun! We will care for Aaron and Mishi while you are gone. Mother, Aaron needs a bath, anyway," said Yael. Katya had been looking forward to some time alone with Eliza. Eliza wanted her mother to sit with her as she read her first scroll from Uncle Cornelius. Katya kissed one daughter goodbye, grabbed the other one's hand, walked down the stairs, and didn't stop until they reached the sea.

Eliza and Katya held hands the entire time as they walked down onto the sand by the sea. Katya asked Eliza many questions about what it was like to be a rabbi in training and what it was like to care for refugees constantly. Eliza answered her as best she could, but she was more focused on getting some time with her mom. They walked up and down the dock system and Eliza introduced her mother to many of the shopkeepers that she knew. Many people offered condolences and the mood was somber. Eventually, they reached a point at a place where the harbor turned and stopped at a small park that Caleb had constructed the first month on the job. It was meant as a place to visit and pray before and after people traveled on the open seas. Men would seldom admit that they were scared to travel on water so big that they could not see the other side. As such, there were benches and trees for the men to sit and reflect on. In the middle of the park was a large piece of marble with a phrase from the Torah engraved in all known languages. Most westward voyages departed in the morning to take advantage of wind direction. Therefore, the marble block sat at an angle so the sun would shine on it when the words were read.

> *So therefore, do not be afraid. I will provide*
> *for you and your little ones.*

Next to the marble was a pile of dirt. Men often took a handful of dirt with them as they boarded their boats and held them during their long periods at sea when they were scared. It would reassure them that life is not all water, despite most of the world being covered with water. The warm loam was reassuring and Caleb made sure that there were baskets of dirt delivered to the park weekly. Eliza released her mother's hand and spoke first as she picked up some of the dirt, explaining to her mother why it was there.

"Mother, I love this place. Uncle and auntie took me here soon after Caleb and Yael moved in with them. Uncle would buy me an orange, peel it, and give it to me while we talked. He was very quiet, but I knew he loved me," she said. Eliza stood up, looked out over the open water, and wiped her hands. She was fidgeting and her mother saw her anxiety.

"Sit back down, Little One. Tell me what is in your heart," said her mom, and she took out an orange from her cloak and began to peel it. Eliza smiled.

"You already knew?"

"No, but Val did." Eliza looked down at the orange and laughed as a lesson from marriage appeared as a gift. Val and Cornelius paid attention when the other talked.

"Cornelius didn't hide everything from Val," Eliza said as she waited for her mother to finish peeling the orange. She then split it in half and they each sat and quietly began to eat it. Katya marveled at the sounds of the ocean waves against the rocks and heard the seagulls as they flew over the sandy coast. Eliza finished her first wedge before speaking to her mother.

"This is where I told them all the details of what happened to Aunt Yael and Uncle Mishi," she said. Her mother reached over and held her hand, not trying to hide the fact that she was crying.

Eliza told her mother all the details of the attack on the school and how Caleb tried to defend everyone. She told her mother how her aunt lost her arm in a sword strike by a soldier and then was killed in the next one. She had to stop and start her tale a few different times as she ate orange wedges.

"Mother, I never told you everything that happened in Rome. Now that we have the time and a beautiful place, it is time you knew." Eliza said as she finished the last orange wedge. She quickly walked to the sea to wash her hands, and she came back.

It took an hour to cover all the details of their trip. She told her how on the boat ride there, she was held down by three men who tried to rape her. Caleb killed two of them and scared the third. She talked about her paralysis when they ran aground and she had to jump into the sea and swim to shore holding a sheep's bladder. She talked about the suffering Caleb experienced when he fought in the Coliseum and he was forced to choose between Yael and her or two men of Yeshua. She talked about how he would have nightmares on the boat ride home, swearing to exact revenge against the emperor. She told her how Titus pulled down her robes, exposing all of her upper body to everyone in the Coliseum. She told her how embarrassed she was to expose her bare chest to a crowd of 70,000 laughing Roman citizens.

Yet she found joy in telling her mother about the other parts of the day that were overlooked.

"Mother, the more I look back on that day, the cloudier it is. It was a day of evil, but all of us got Yael from that sickness. I knew nothing about her, yet it was so easy to give away Caleb's winning to buy her freedom. I knew she was trustworthy and didn't deserve to be there. I also sensed that Yeshua would do great things with her and for her if I would sacrifice to save her first. Now she is Caleb's wife and one of my best friends."

Her mother smiled at her and reached out to rub her head.

"I could not be prouder of you for investing in our beautiful Yael. Your inner beauty exceeds your outer beauty, perhaps more than anyone I have known, Little One." Eliza bowed her head in respect for her mother. When she finally looked up, Katya finished her thought.

"I think you may be more beautiful on the inside than your aunt!" Eliza said. Eliza was not ready to receive such a compliment from her mother. Dor had told her that she needed to let herself be loved by someone other than Caleb. Instead, she shifted topics in her awkwardness.

"Uncle did well teaching her how to read and write Greek. Her written Ebreet is excellent, too. We all know her ministry is on the top of that mountain, but I wonder, Mother. Perhaps she could be a teacher," Eliza speculated.

"That will work itself out. Just let things unfold. But I have wondered the same thing. She is an excellent teacher to the servants' children. I have been watching her teach them when they come into the kitchen. She plays games with them as they learn the alphabet," Katya said. Eliza hadn't been paying attention and didn't know that.

"Mother, Uncle Cornelius and Aunt Valentina were upset that Caleb and I experienced so much loss at a young age. I think that is why they spent so much time holding the three of us. Now I understand what they were doing. He was giving us a safe touch. Cornelius and Val touched us to help us overcome the damaging touch done by others." Katya nodded and liked her daughter's insight. After another pause, Katya spoke.

"I adopted Yael as my own, treating her like I treat you. But I birthed you, and you will also have a special place in my heart that no one else shares. I love you and am proud that you followed in my sister's footsteps. She would also be very proud of you." After that, the two just sat there looking at the waves in the distance.

"Mother, this little piece of Caesarea is a place of cleansing for me. I could think of no place to go where I could tell you everything. That is why I want to read Uncle's scroll here."

"Go ahead," her mother said.

"OK!" she said as she broke the sealed scroll and anxiously read the first line. She knew Uncle Cornelius did not write as he spoke, and she expected this to be a bit more formal than she was used to. She did not skim it but immediately started speaking.

*From Cornelius, Tribute of Caesarea, servant of Titus and Yeshua*
*To: Emperor Titus, son of Vespasian, our Caesar*

*"Congratulations, young man, on becoming our Emperor in this great Empire. You are now the most powerful man in the world. Val and I celebrated with a cup of wine when we received the news, as she and I have known you since you were a young boy playing with our son Rufus. Hopefully, my son will be next to you as the Senate confirms your place as our leader and places the crown upon your head. Perhaps more than ever, you will need your boyhood friends as you begin your reign in the most treacherous city in the history of the world. Remember, when life in Rome becomes crazy, you always have a safe place to stay at our home in Caesarea. The same room over our kitchen that you slept in as a boy is here for you. As I write this, I am in my basement, a few steps away from the woman who cooked what you used to call the best tasting bread in all the empire.*

*As you know, all tribunes and Legates take a moment to write a letter or personally visit the Emperor and the Senate when leadership changes. Many of us spend our careers seeking more significant positions in the military, and I can only imagine that many of my peers will come and seek an audience with you. Perhaps you have already received visitors to the Palatine Hills. Take care and know this. My wife and I will not come to you to seek political gain. If we come to see you, we will eat with you and watch the sunset together. When you arrive here in Caesarea, Val will make the bread just the way you like it, and I will make sure we have fresh game and some spirits to drink as we watch the sunset from our rooftop. More than once, you fell asleep on our pillows on the roof after dinner and sunset, and I carried you to bed to lay you down to sleep. Although you are too big for me to carry you down the stairs, Val and I both talk about that time and miss you."*

"Mother, did you know any of this? Titus used to come here!"

"No, if anyone knew, it would have been Caleb's father. He talked to Rufus more than anyone else. Perhaps Caleb knows," she said with a shrug.

"Well, Caleb did not mention to me that the emperor slept on the roof!" she said. Then, she continued her reading.

*"However, I now take ownership of a new role in your education that I fear most will dare not embark upon. I need to tell you a story that continues to prove true and will forever change the empire. So, you know, I originally did not believe it. As our leader and my adopted son, I want to tell you the story of a Messiah named Yeshua who came into the world. Many of his followers are within a stone's throw of you now, and I suspect that many of the slaves and servants in your palace are his followers. Before you react, let me educate you.*

*First, these followers call themselves members of 'the way' and they mean you no harm and have no intention of usurping your position. They do not seek to overthrow the Empire. Indeed, I am perhaps the greatest Roman citizen who also claims loyalty to Yeshua as he does to you, Caesar. If any attempt to challenge you or take your life, consider me the traitor and take my head instead. I offer myself as their collateral.*

*Second, you must listen to this with an open mind. The followers of Yeshua are praying for you. I am with them in that we pray that you are open to the idea that Yeshua's message applies to you as much as it does to me, my servants, and my children.*

*I must elaborate on why we pray to this Messiah and worship him and not the gods of old. You would find this tale unbelievable if it did not come from me, and it has been in my heart to tell you about this since I first heard that you were now our emperor.*

*I have been blessed with the language of the people I govern. For thousands of years, these Ebreet have spoken of a foretelling of a Messiah coming to the world to save them from oppression that has always defined their history. Their God often sent a servant, a prophet, a plague, and other unbelievable events to save them. However, this Messiah was different than any who came before him. His appearance was anticipated, but many Ebreet people thought this Messiah would free them from what they describe as bondage to our Empire.*

*Hopefully, you remember the afternoon you and Rufus chased down a deer and you cornered it, not knowing it was pregnant. When it paused from its attempts to run and save its own life, it laid down and delivered its baby. I remember how you walked back onto the courtyard late that afternoon. The two of you told me how you stood in wonder, looking at the newborn fawn stand for the first time, and began nursing from a highly fatigued mother. You both came home and spoke nearly nothing at dinner when I asked you about the shame you felt chasing down what was the most magnificent birth either of you had witnessed.*

*If I remember, you told me that you had no idea what was about to happen. Once you discovered what was about to happen, your view of the mother and the terrain became insignificant as you stared at that baby and saw how it gave the mother hope. You both called it magnificent. You were mesmerized watching the animal stand for the first time.*

*My emperor, that birth has occurred. This fawn's name was Yeshua. This Messiah came to save them from the death that comes from sin. In the same way, you chased the mother down, unaware of what was about to happen, I, too, have done things I did not wish to do. Through this struggle, the Messiah came to free us, both Ebreet and Roman. This Messiah came to tell us that no man or government is our enemy. The real enemy is our sin.*

*I have examined the recorded history of his life and the stories of those who follow him, and he lived a life without sin. Then, he sacrificed himself to pay for all of our sins. Just like we place young virgin girls to appease the Gods during times of trouble, this Messiah represents the eternal sacrifice such that no one else must atone any longer. He is our atonement.*

*He has also sent a powerful messenger among us called the Holy Spirit. I have many experiences with this Holy Spirit, and I believe that one day, he will also come upon you, and you will know who he is. It may originate from an esteemed empire member like me, but this Holy Spirit gave me a prophecy gift.*

*I see that it will come from a young Ebreet girl with a story to tell that you cannot resist."*

Eliza's opened her eyes as wide as she could and raised her voice. "Mother, did you hear that?" she rhetorically asked.

"Just keep reading, Eliza," she said. Katya remained calm, but she felt joy in seeing how her daughter was seeing her destiny unfold in front of her.

> *"Be aware, my emperor, that this Messiah's message will come to you again and again, and soon, it will take over your heart as it did mine. You will sense when this Ebreet girl is upon you, and you will change in front of her. Your old self will die. The sins that have infected your soul will suddenly disappear once you meet her.*
>
> *It is blasphemy to say this, and I know that my life is forfeit according to the rules of our Senate, but I follow Yeshua's teachings with all my heart. And I tell you the truth; the Empire is better for it. I continue to collect taxes, manage crime, and keep the empire growing at rates above your expectations. Just like I would die for the Empire, I would also die for Yeshua.*
>
> *I know that you are committed to finishing the great Coliseum that your father started. I hope it serves your legacy well. I would like to see it with you one day and tell you more about the Messiah. Please send an invitation to Val and I, and we will accept it immediately.*
>
> *Val and I love you very much. We are very proud of you."*

Cornelius' seal was at the bottom. Eliza let the scroll roll up and put it back in her bag.

"I am not shocked by any of that," said Katya.

"I am!" said Eliza, uncertain how to express her overwhelming sense of humility.

"It makes sense that he gave you that! The young girl in the letter is you!" she said. Eliza knew that, but she could not fathom the depth of its meaning yet.

"Do you remember learning from your auntie how Yeshua's mother was unassuming yet chosen by Yahweh to carry the Messiah to the world? I always thought you had the same disposition as Marion might have had. I asked, "Did Yahweh know that my daughter would share the greatest story ever told to the emperor of Rome and see him believe?" she said.

"Mother, this is inconceivable to me." She stared out over the ocean then turned back to her mother.

"Mother, how did Uncle Cornelius know that I would be the one to carry the message to the emperor? That was not my intention as I sailed on the boat to seek his help freeing you and father from slavery," she said. Tears began flowing down her face and her mother did what she always did, drawing her near her, holding her head to her chest, and letting her cry while she rubbed her head.

"Little One, that is why I have always thought of you as I think of Marion. She was also sincerely humble while the calling on her life was disclosed, just like you are now. Doesn't that story give you faith that the Holy Spirit is using you for big things? And his isn't done yet, I tell you!" she said. She held her daughter's face in her hands and looked her directly in the eyes.

"You are learning how precious you are and I get to be part of it. For now, we should get back. I am sure your little brother is now hungry, and I am his milk source."

# Chapter 12:
# Coming back together

Once Eliza and Katya climbed back up the stairs to the family compound, they walked directly to the kitchen. In Ebreet culture, important decisions and conversations happen in the kitchen. Katya was grateful for her time with her daughter but baby Aaron needed her. She took a seat next to Yael at the kitchen table and nursed her baby boy. Caleb had been training all morning and had just bathed. His beard and hair were wet, but he joined the rest of his family to talk about the contents of Eliza's scroll. Eliza summarized it as her mother listened and Katya wore a smile of joy as her daughter unveiled the prophecy that foretold of a young Ebreet girl leading the Emperor of Rome to a belief in a risen Messiah. Eliza fluffed her hair as a sign of royalty and pride.

"Duh, stupid. We already knew that," said Caleb, in the traditional derogatory tone that he used as she stated what he thought was obvious.

"Oh, Caleb, please be nice. I was there, and your cousin was riveting to watch. You know you are just jealous," said Yael.

"No, I am not jealous! I hated every part of that day. Remember, I killed two brothers that day," he said without hesitation.

Yael had heard enough and she threw the iron pot that she was cooking with. Everyone stopped talking as it was obvious she was mad.

"Would you two stop? We all have good reasons to be resentful of the emperor, as do literally hundreds of thousands of our people. Instead, we are doing this?" she said, using a scolding look on her face as she made eye contact with each of them.

"If Uncle Cornelius were still here, he would say you two are competing for the donkey of the day medallion!" she said, which made everyone laugh.

"You guys had it bad for exactly one day! I got raped for months!" she said, changing her baby from one side to the other. Caleb and Eliza bowed their heads in shame. They apologized to Yael and they sat quietly, allowing Yael a chance to speak.

"I remember from my time with the royal family. They thought they knew everything. I could not dream that he might listen to the story of a Messiah. I was sure no person, regardless of experience, would convince him of anything. He had to learn things for himself. I cannot tell you how often I heard him talk about how much he hated the Senate and how people without experience thought they knew everything. Eliza, you were the right person at the right time. It was Caleb's toughness in combat that made all of that possible," she added. She told a few anecdotal tales to make her point and everyone laughed at how immature the conversations within the royal palace could be. Once she was done, Caleb asked Eliza a question.

"Cousin, Can I read your scroll?" asked Caleb. Eliza was tempted to say, "If I can read yours," but she needed to trust that Caleb knew what was best for her. He said he couldn't tell her about his scroll and she needed to accept that truth.

"Sure," she said. She handed it to him, and he opened it and turned around. While he quietly read it, Eliza and Yael had a light conversation about dinner. After Caleb finished, he handed it back to Eliza, shaking his head.

"Eliza, I am sorry. God has a plan for you that is still being revealed. Please forgive me for what I said," he said.

"So, I am not stupid after all?" she said playfully.

"I didn't say that. I merely apologized," said Caleb, matching her playfulness. She leaned over and kissed him on the cheek as she always did after they had a verbal joust. As soon as they reconciled, Yael spoke up.

"Eliza, I spent a lot of time in the basement. I am pretty sure there is a second letter to the emperor that he left for you," Yael added.

"OK, I need your help finding it," she said, obviously enthusiastic about what else Cornelius had to say.

Eliza chimed in with a new thought.

"All of us have already lived a lifetime. Do you think that the paths we travel are ones we chose, or do you think they were ordained for us by God?" she asked. They had all thought about that but not discussed it.

"I do not believe God meant for me to watch my parents get murdered or to learn that my wife was raped. No, we are traveling a path our parents and grandparents chose for us," Caleb added.

Yael added her opinion.

"I feel that much of the path I have taken I did not choose. Once you two arrived in the Coliseum, I had no way of knowing that day would change my life's direction. All I did that day was support the two of you. I shot no arrows, I told no stories, and I shared no love of Yeshua with the emperor. All I did was stand near you and pray. There is no way to understand that you would be my sister and you would be my husband," she said, pointing at Eliza and Caleb, respectively.

"And you would adopt me as your daughter," she said, pointing at Katya.

"Yet here I am! My reward for faithfulness was to see my dreams come true," she added, looking down at her sleeping child and then up at her gorgeous and completely committed husband.

"That is the power of humble prayer," said Eliza, with a melancholic look on her face.

Eliza knew she needed to table her jealousy, but Eliza and Katya could see it in her demeanor. Yael had a much harder life than she did, growing up a poor farmer's daughter. Eliza grew up in a small village, but everyone there was extremely wealthy due to the gold present in the hills where they lived. Eliza's needs were always met. Except that now, the poor farmer's daughter had a husband and a child, and the rich girl had neither and she wanted both.

She could not shake that truth. She knew she was following her calling to be a rabbi, yet she wished for what Yael had. She desired a husband and children, but she did not talk about it. Like her sister, she knew she needed to stand, pray, and trust Yahweh with the outcome. It was time for her to voice her opinion on this matter.

"I think we all get to choose our path. I certainly could have kept my mouth closed when I sat with the emperor, and I could easily have agreed to let the emperor have his way with me in exchange for protecting Caleb from harm. I could have said 'no' to Dor after he called me to become his disciple. I could have instead taken a husband, had children, and lived out my days in my family's village. I don't say this often, but I am jealous of Yael. She has a husband and a child, and I want both of those things. I have chosen otherwise. I say we have a choice in our outcomes," she said with authority.

"A good man will come your way and ask you to enter Erusin. I pray for it all the time," said Caleb.

Katya added her opinion as well.

"When your father and I were enslaved and working on the reparations on the walls of Jerusalem, we saw many atrocities that I don't need to describe. We lacked adequate clothing to keep warm and I lost knowledge of what the rest of my family was doing. I had just seen my sister and her husband killed, and my husband had been beaten to a pulp. Yet your father and I have talked about this repeatedly over these years. He and I have been more connected because of the time we spent as slaves. We looked forward to seeing each other at the end of the day more than when we were newly married and trying to have a family. We may not have had much choice regarding our situation, but we had great choices with our attitude. Each time we saw something awful come to pass, I could still thank Yahweh for the gift of life. I looked forward to my husband coming back to me each night." She rocked her child as she finished her tale.

"You know, I am blessed beyond words. I have two lovely, grown-up daughters, and this beautiful baby boy in my arms is a dream come true. I have a grandson, too. This must feel like heaven. Your father feels the same way I do. He works hard to care for all of us. He loves you girls greatly. Your father shows off whenever he can tell people about the two of you. Do you know what he says? He says that his oldest daughter is married to the centurion of Caesarea and his youngest is a teacher in the line of Melchizedek. He is crazy about you girls!" Katya paused to reposition her baby before she continued. Once Aaron latched back onto her breast, she continued.

"If I were to lose your father today, I would always look back at my life as a slave as a wonderful time, full of love. Your father has never loved me more," she said.

The girls looked at their mother, wondering if they would achieve her levels of gratitude and wisdom.

"Mother, what should we tell our children about my time or your time as a slave?" Yael asked. Aaron had finished feeding and she was now burping him.

"Nothing until they ask. Just as you three are now open to hearing stories about the times that your father and I had at the wall, your child will prompt you as the moment presents itself. You will feel comfortable sharing about your trip to Rome, your battles, and your readings of these scrolls from Cornelius. All you need to do is be patient and pray. Yeshua will do the demanding work for you." Katya had another point to add.

"You know what your father and I did while we lived at the wall? We wrote a prayer for you and your children. Slavery reminded us that our lives will fade one day. During the cold nights, your father and I shared a single blanket to stay warm. We prayed for our children and your children together. Yes, we prayed for little Mishi before Yael and Caleb conceived him! Though we did not know Caleb as a son-in-law or Yael as an adopted daughter, we prayed that God would allow us to parent whatever children came into our lives. Literally, the morning after we said that part of our prayer, we were free to go. That is the time you three came and had us released from slavery. Yahweh heard our new prayer and answered it."

"There are hundreds of scrolls in the basement. He made copies of everything. We will be here for a month reading them all," Eliza said.

"I am sure uncle knew that. He gave us what he thought we needed for this time in our lives. The rest will always be there, and you can come back and read them any time you like," said Caleb. The weather was nice and all the women stepped outside to spend time in the warming sun.

Caleb sat quietly in his kitchen and did not take the day off from work as he had the day before. Two of his lieutenants entered the compound and approached him. He saw them coming and he excused himself. He found himself involved in work-related issues for the rest of the afternoon. His men told him that he was needed at the harbor. He nodded his cloak, which signified he was the centurion and adjusted the brooch to be in the center. He put his helmet on and walked toward the iron gate entrance and the stairs leading to the rest of the city.

"I will be back at dinner," he said. He took two steps away before turning around and returning to his mother-in-law. He leaned over and kissed her on the cheek.

"Thank you for your prayers," he said. Katya knew what to say.

"Your mother would be enormously proud of the man you have become, Caleb," she said.

Eliza gazed into the distance as her cousin walked away. Yael was right. Caleb's mother would be proud of the man he has become. She knew he was bound to her for life, even though that was not recorded in the prophecy. She and Caleb would share the same path many times over the decades to come.

# Chapter 13:
# The Scroll Meant for all

Caleb returned from work and appeared to be in good spirits. People came into his office all day offering condolences and he didn't get much work done. His lieutenant David saw that his leader was distracted and he took over some tasks that he normally didn't do to make sure Caleb could speak to people who showed concern for his well-being.

When he left, he thanked David repeatedly, inviting him and his family to join them for Shabbat. As he climbed the stairs to his compound, he carried with him the burden of this morning's scroll. He could already see a good place to apply his uncle's teachings. He was very excited to come home to what was now his mountaintop villa to be with his favorite woman in the world. He wanted to let all the women in his life know that he was their protector. He kissed his wife first, then he moved down the line, kissing his mother-in-law, aunt, and cousin in that order. He then thanked Yael for doing a wonderful job at maintaining their home and he took Mishi for a walk.

Once dinner was over, Yael handed Eliza another scroll.

"This one is meant for all of us," she said. Her smile made it obvious that she had already read it and Eliza yanked it from her hands with a sense of jealousy. Eliza opened the scroll, looked up at her sister, and started laughing immediately.

*"Eliza, my dear, I know you have heard Luke's
version of what happened in your aunt's handwriting. What do you say about hearing the story from*

*me? I was the man in the story, after all! Ha. You can share this with anyone and everyone. Enjoy! I still laugh as I read this."*

"The date of the letter was a few months ago," Eliza said.

"Duh! He couldn't write his own story before it happened, could he?" Caleb could not pass up a good joke. Eliza stuck her tongue out at Caleb and laughed, too.

Then Eliza began to read out loud.

*"I certainly have not been sleeping well lately. Val is having the same problem. We wake up in the middle of the night and talk about these visions we are having. I don't know exactly when they started but it has been going on for months. It started sometime after I got promoted and began integrating with these local people and attending their synagogue. Now that the mystery of these dreams has been revealed, I must write them down.*

*Some months ago, Val convinced me we needed to invest our time in integrating with this community. One afternoon, my wife's friends from the harbor markets invited us to Beit Knesset the following evening. It means 'house of gathering' in the Ebreet tongue, but everyone calls it 'synagogue' when we are walking around town. We visited their gathering a few times and decided that we liked the people and how sincere everyone appeared. We formally joined them, and we commonly hear someone say, 'See you at Beit Knesset,' when we pass them in the markets now.*

*So far, the synagogue has been the best place to meet local people and spend time with them. The rabbi knows who I am outside of the synagogue and his rebbetzin shops with Val on Shabbat. Val finds it interesting to learn what being married to a Rabbi is like. Her husband is always teaching and reading words that are hundreds of years old. We are learning history not taught at the schools in Rome and we are hearing about all the changes in land ownership that have happened since the Ebreet crossed the river and took possession of the land 2,000 years ago. People are patient with us as we practice using the new language and they are quick to offer us kind words, a warm drink, and non-judgmental ears. They can sense when we are tired and sometimes allow us to rest and unwind when we are with them, not asking anything of us. Sometimes, I don't know what I would do without the safety I feel in the synagogue each week. Val says I come home in peace, no matter how I felt when I entered.*

*I called it 'temple' once, but some old men graciously corrected me. I heard Titus and Rufus both talk about the temple where Jews gathered, but I didn't know the meaning. After all, no one corrects a centurion! They taught me that there are many synagogues but one temple. It was at that moment that I was convinced they didn't see me as a centurion but as a man who wished to fear Yahweh, just like they did. I wanted to tell them that the temple they referred to was destroyed by my son Rufus and his best friend, Titus, the former emperor. I decided that the truth would not endear me to them or them to me. Val said it was a good idea to keep my mouth shut. Despite all these accolades I am recording, these Ebreet are a crazy lot. For example, a few older men came to me and said that the temple would be rebuilt one day. We will see, but I will wager it won't happen in my lifetime. Ha.*

*The room where we gather could be better lit, but it feels as inviting as home. There are lots of hugs and kisses as we enter, and I don't feel like the battering arm of the Roman Empire when I am there. I am just another face in the crowd and Val thinks it makes me a better man when I am not seen as a governor of a Roman city. The rabbi has impressed upon me that I have been greatly blessed with wealth since I was promoted to centurion. Val and I have agreed to tithe one out of ten coins I earn to the mission of the synagogue. I also come once per month and help prepare food for the homeless on the docks and I require my lieutenants to do the same thing. Of course, most of them do not like it, but Hyaenas is the youngest one, and he does.*

*These visions continued to upset our sleep and they reached a high point one afternoon. I came home from work earlier than normal and Val and I greeted each other when we saw a vision in front of us. It spoke out loud, but neither of us was scared. He said to us,*

*'Your prayers and gifts to the poor have come as a blessing before Yahweh. Now send men to Joppa to bring back a man named Simon Peter. He is staying in a tanner's house. The tanner's name is also Simon. It is near the sea.'*

*Val looked at me and said, 'Is this our burning bush?' We both laughed. Perhaps it was because I was a disciplined soldier that took away any sense of fear I might have. Certainly, this was not an adversary speaking to us, so it made no sense to be scared. The next morning, I sent Hyaenas and two servants to find Simon Peter and bring him back. When I gave them the name and told them to go to Joppa, they were very sarcastic, reminding me how big Joppa is, how many people named Simon live there, and how many houses are by the sea. They said it would have been easier to find water in a desert than to find a tanner in a city living by the sea. Yet they found him!*

*Before Simon Peter arrived in Caesarea, I invited many of our new family members from the synagogue to be with us. Something about me could sense Peter was on the stairs and I became weak. Once he stepped into our compound, I fell at his feet. He told me to stand up and then he began his conversation with me, which lasted for many days. At first, he said,*

*'You know that it is against our law for an Ebreet to associate with or visit a gentile spiritually. But God has shown me that I should not call anyone impure or unclean.' He said more things that I don't remember and then he asked me why I sent the men to get him. I told him that Val and I had seen an angel. He asked about the angel and I described him as a man in shining clothes who appeared in my compound in the middle of the day, but he did not come through the gate where my guards stood. I repeated everything the angel said to us. I also told him that Val and I were already attending synagogue. I told him that the people here have already accepted me as one of their own.*

*Peter said, 'I now realize how true it is that God does not show favorites but accepts from every nation the ones who fear him and do what is right. You know the message Yahweh sent to the people of Judah, announcing the good news of Peace through Yeshua, the Messiah, who is Adonai of all.'*

*He said many things after that, but I can't recall them accurately enough to write them here. He spoke incessantly about Yeshua and how he came to save us from our sins. Before he could finish his tale, an unseen messenger arrived in our midst, and many from the synagogue began speaking in tongues, singing, and praising Yeshua. The rabbi and his Rebbetzin spoke in a foreign language; others translated what was said back into Greek for all to understand.*

*These next words I write are perhaps the craziest part of the experience for me. While many who spoke in tongues could not maintain that language once Peter left, Val and I did. From that moment forward, Val and I could speak Ebreet as if it were our mother tongue. I could also read it. In fact, after Peter left, I went to the synagogue on a day when no one was there, and I asked the rabbi to open the scrolls. The rabbi knew I was new to the faith and he held the scrolls open while I read and spoke the words on the parchment. The rabbi was shocked that I spoke as quickly as he could and that my pronunciation was perfect. I considered writing this letter in Ebreet to make my point. I have not been to an Ebreet school, yet I can read any Ebreet text you place in front of me, including the oldest of documents.*

*We all went down to the sea and Peter baptized many of us. He stayed with me for a few days and we all gathered at the synagogue each evening after the day's work was complete. We stayed late learning about the Messiah.*

*Peter taught us many things that day but also told us of his failures. He cried from the depths of his soul as he recalled how he rejected the Messiah three times, as had been foretold to him. He also told us with great shame how he lost his faith while walking on water and required rescue. And he knew that he had a habit of drinking too much wine.*

*Peter told us that Yeshua would return, but no one knew when that would happen. On the last night we were together, he told me on the walk back up the stairs to our compound that he would be leaving in the morning. I asked him when he was returning, but he didn't know. He said he would send messengers to check on our congregation. Then he stopped and looked me in the eye. He told me that my story of meeting the unseen messenger would be a part of history for all times sake, on par with the story of David and Goliath in its importance to the history of the world. He said that it would be more important than any Caesar, and the tales of our meeting would last for thousands of years to come. Val told me not to let it get to my head and she jokingly slapped my face to make her point. Yet each time she and I talk to each other in Ebreet without realizing we are using this language, we are reminded that whatever Peter said must be true. Surely, all of what has happened to us is impossible. Yet it happened.*

*My problems are compounded by my inability to do as Peter taught us. Just like he failed Yeshua, so did I. I go to work each day but do evil things. There has not been a single week since Peter has left that I have not felt shame at what I am required to do. Indeed, what Peter said about my history haunts me. Will people everywhere read tales of Cornelius the Crucifier and Cornelius the slaver? Certainly, I spend more time doing those acts than attending the synagogue or helping the needy. If these acts define me and are to be a part of history, I fear for those who must read them.*

*May God forgive my evil heart.*

"That is a sad ending!" said Eliza. Caleb, too, was shaking his head. He knew Cornelius in a different light than this story describes. Yael knew better than to leave everyone in a depressed state.

"I am glad that he wrote that for all of us. It is good to know that it agrees with what Luke told us, and it adds some important details."

Eliza stared at everyone, taking a sip of her drink and looking for feedback. She had plenty of words to say, but she needed a rest after reading such a long letter. Caleb remained stoic, perhaps because he saw a little bit of Cornelius in himself.

"Are you going to make a copy of it?" asked her mother.

"I don't know. I certainly will tell others about it. This is a missing piece of history. It sounds like the story of the ancient prophets, except that we know the author," Yael said. She raised a finger to get her sister's attention.

"Eliza, how do you know whether something is from Yahweh? You are nearly a rabbi now. How do you know that the Torah is complete or are there missing parts?" Yael asked. Everyone wanted to hear Eliza's answer.

"The words of Yahweh are written not on paper but in our hearts. I have read the Torah many times and believe I have all of it memorized. Yet, not all of it is in my heart. I find that I covet things others have," she said, looking over at her sister and pointing at baby Mishi.

"I also trust that if Yahweh wants the telling of this story to be a part of history, it will happen, regardless of what I think. My job is to listen to Him. He is a living God. He doesn't stop with the words in the Torah. The Torah is where we start to learn about him. It doesn't end there."

"You are wise beyond your years, Little One," said her mother.

Everyone sat in silence for a moment until they heard some commotion outside the gate. It was nearly dark outside but it was obvious that someone had just arrived at the compound. Katya's face lit up. She handed her child to Eliza and ran out the door. Her husband Matthew stepped into view and she jumped up and hugged him. He kissed her and told her he loved her.

"How are my girls?" he said, looking down at the two sitting on the kitchen floor. Each one held a child in their arms.

"Father, we heard you were not coming until tomorrow," said Yael.

"I pushed on. I didn't want to stay at a tavern if I didn't have to," he said. "Stand up and give your father a hug!" he said. Each girl did and he kissed them on their cheeks. He took anointing oil from his belt and put it on each of their foreheads, as tradition dictated. He then spoke a blessing over each of them, as he always did, and gave them another hug.

"I am hungry," he said, and the servants brought out the leftover lamb and some cold bread for him. He gratefully ate it all, graciously accepted a full glass of red wine, and sat as close as he could to his two daughters.

"Tell me what is going on, girls! Tell me everything!" he said.

"Where do we start?" asked Eliza. Everyone laughed.

"I am going to bed. Yael, give me Mishi, and you can stay up and talk," Caleb said.

"I am going with you," said Katya, following Caleb's queue. "Girls, you can have this entire evening with your father. I have had you to myself these last few days. He misses you, too."

# Chapter 14:
# Eliza reads the wrong scroll.

The following morning, it was cold again. Cesarean winters were often like this, with days alternating between beautiful and mild, then windy and cold. Eliza sat next to the outdoor fire with the servants. Eliza was wrapped in a blanket made from Lebanese wool, sipping her tea and eating fresh bread with hummus as the sun rose in the east. Caleb stood behind her, with his hands on her shoulder, looking for David to come up the stairs. The servants were telling jokes and everyone was laughing as life after Cornelius started to take its new form. She had already picked up the next scroll in the basement with her initials on it and was mentally preparing to read it. She wanted to know what happened next in the conversation between Cornelius and Titus. For now, she loved Caleb's touch and she could see how the servants were coping with the loss of their master. She basked in their humor, wondering how she might use their jokes the next time that she preached.

David walked in and greeted everyone. Caleb and David immediately left to go into the city below. The group continued talking at the fireplace until the sun was up enough to warm things and brighten the sky.

"I think I am ready to read this next scroll," Eliza said, getting up and walking up to the rooftop. She kept her blanket as she walked up the stairs and took a seat on her uncle's sofa. Maka, the house cat, saw her, and she jumped up with Eliza and quickly settled into her lap. Eliza petted the cat a few times and spoke to it in Aramaic, as her aunt used to do, then started reading with the scroll in one hand

and her cup of tea in the other. She could not have scripted a better scene to read.

As soon as she opened it, she saw the date and was perplexed. This could not be the second letter to Titus. It was dated much earlier than the last scroll. Regardless, it had her name, so she continued to read it. All she knew was that it had her initials on it. She pressed down the parchment with one hand and held her tea in the other, this time making sure not to spill it.

> *"It has been three months since Peter left me. He made mention of going to Rome. The port master told me yesterday evening that he had made a deposit on a charter to Rome three weeks ago, but it appears that he decided to travel to Jerusalem instead. I don't know why.*
>
> *A report came yesterday from Jerusalem and it showed his name as one of those recently arrested. It doesn't list the reason. I am now both angry at him and scared for him. I said nothing to my men or family when I saw his name on the list, but as I walked back up the hill to our compound, I asked myself, 'What did that short, fat man do to justify Rome's wrath?' Something seemed wrong about this arrest and I decided to deal with it myself.*
>
> *However, I knew it was possible that he did, in fact, break Roman law and set himself up to be punished.*
>
> *As I walked up the stairs, I imagined him retelling his tales. His stories are incredible to the layman, especially when the Holy Spirit doesn't prepare the listener's heart. He likely angered the Pharisees. They might have thought he was another lunatic seeking to upset their authority. I suspect I can have this event rewritten as a misunderstanding in the arrest record, but I need to get to Jerusalem*

*before he gets hung on a cross. The administrators there love using their crosses!*

*In the past, Peter's words kept me awake at night. Immediately after he left, the scroll he gave me made me excited to wake up in the morning and read. Now, this! He opens his mouth without thinking and this is what happens. If I could slap him right now, I would do it!*

*I wrote and sent this letter two days ago, and I am leaving for Jerusalem on horseback tomorrow to make sure that my word reaches the right ears. I am taking two of my lieutenants and a part of my regiment with me. I may need to escort him from prison forcefully. Politically, this is complicated. I do not know this new person in charge of the city, Marcus Agrippa. He refers to himself as King of Judaea, but we all know that he isn't.*

**To: Marcus Agrippa, the great leader of Jerusalem**
**From: Cornelius, Centurion of Caesarea, the great coastal port of Rome in Judah**

**Long live the Empire! Let me welcome you to this land as one of the oldest Roman residents in Judah. Judah has been my family's home for over a decade. Over these next five years, while you serve your term, I look forward to getting to know you and your family.**

**Our leaders in Rome have empowered us to rule over sizable portions of the Empire. As you know, I protect one of our main ports from chaos and bandits that take from our profits and stability. Few of us in charge keep the peace and remain in control of the threats that endanger the empire without open communi-**

cations with each other. As such, I am coming to see you for our conversation regarding the governance of this land.

I have seen written that you may have accidentally imprisoned an Ebreet named Simon Peter. He is dear to the people of my house. I hide nothing and am sending a copy of this letter to Caesar to ensure no one misinterprets my words.

This man named Peter was a discipline of Yeshua of Nazareth and from personal experience, I can tell you he means no harm to the empire. A few months ago, I met Simon Peter in the courtyard of my family's compound. Peter was sent to me and spent many days with my family. He told us many stories of the appearance of Yeshua, the Messiah of both the Ebreet people and Roman citizens. I was convicted and followed up on his claims.

Peter's words and actions have changed my life and my mission as a Centurion. I am a better man because of him, and the people I govern are better off, as I use his teachings in many of my decisions. I am aware that he has a propensity for telling unbelievable stories and he has demonstrated the capacity to drink too much wine on occasion. That said, Peter gives people hope and poses no threat to Rome. Indeed, when he left me, I had a feeling of peace that I did not experience as a soldier. I have written and spoken to Caesar about this peace, and I openly challenge you to hear his stories without bias. This man must be set free.

If you wish to free him before I arrive, please make it appear that some angel has freed him from prison. This would be the eas-

**iest solution for the Romans and the Pharisees to hear as they accepted his release.**
**Stamp of the Centurion**

*As I prepare to travel to the City of David, I wonder what will become of my life as I commit to saving this man from what might be a horrible death. He will most likely make future mistakes and end up being crucified for something that was not criminal. Assuredly, he will not receive a fair trial. I will do what I can, but there is only so much a Centurion can do. After all, it is not a war against the rulers of this world that we fight. It is a battle of spirits that causes changes in outcomes in our world.*

*After I wrote that letter, one of the merchants who frequently sailed up and down the coast told me they heard of a time when Peter called on the Holy Spirit to bring a little girl back to life. A different merchant, who slipped down from him on the docks, said he saw Peter in Lydda when he met a humble man named Aeneas. Aeneas was paralyzed and had been bedridden for eight years. Peter told him to stand up and walk, and he did. Interestingly, Peter refused to take credit for any of these miracles but instead gave all the glory to Yeshua. More importantly, he did not think it was worth his time to tell me, though I now served as his protectorate in the Empire. This man seeks no glory when it would serve many people to take it. I don't see how this faith can survive with men in charge who keep their marketing successes a secret worthy of hiding. Why did Yeshua pick him? It is a poor choice from my position.*

*When I reached Jerusalem, Agrippa had already released him, and no one knew where he had gone.*

*I would love to see Peter again and learn what happened here. Agrippa offered me no insight. I am reminded that we do not get to control who comes and goes in our lives. All these earthly relationships are temporary. I bit my tongue in front of Agrippa and extended gratitude for his willingness to let the man go unharmed. We ate our first meal together and I listened to his tales until I had heard enough. Hopefully, he will get promoted and return to Rome in a season or two.*

*Perhaps one day Peter will return to see me. I already pray for this. I have already started a list of questions I would like him to answer when he returns. I might see him on the trip here, but that hope was taken away today.*

*My questions for Peter:*

*How do I reconcile the law of Moses with the law of the Messiah?*

*How do I love Jehovah and his people if my job is to force them into compliance with the rule of Rome?*

*How do I teach the men around me who seek promotion and professional growth that they must be willing to die on the cross daily when, instead, we put people on the cross to die daily?*

*I need help. Oh, I need help.*

Eliza looked ahead and spoke aloud as she finished. She wasn't aware that her mother was now next to her, holding baby Aaron. Eliza had no idea that she was crying; all she could sense was the warmth of the housecat and the now cold cup of tea.

"Honey, what in that scroll upset you?" Kayta asked.

"Mother, Cornelius sounds like Caleb did on the boat ride back from Rome. This scroll was meant for him, I think," she said. She began rolling it up as her mother chimed in.

"I think not. Your uncle was very deliberate. Although the content was perhaps more like Caleb's story, it was certainly meant for you to glean from," she said.

"He was wasting his time. I don't know what it is like to walk in either of their sandals, and I realistically never will. I am not a warrior," she said.

"Perhaps that is why he gave it to you. He saw that you needed to know about his life for a reason," her mother said.

"Why? I am not taking the path of a warrior or a great leader." Eliza said. Katya smiled.

"Today, I agree with your cousin. You are stupid and blind to what everyone else sees. Eliza, you already are a great leader," she said, reaching out and holding her daughter's cheek.

Eliza reached down and petted the cat again. Maka was already asleep and had long since stopped purring. Touching the animal brought her back to a place that was truthful and made sense. Those who rest find peace. Maka had long since figured that out. Eliza took a deep breath in and let it out.

"Thank you, Mother. I needed to hear that from you. Maybe that is why Uncle gave me that scroll, after all."

# Chapter 15:
# Two tales for Yael of
# early marriage living

Mishi was finally asleep from his morning nap, and everyone else around the compound was doing something. Yael finally had a few moments, and she decided it was her turn to read one of her uncle's letters. She walked up to the rooftop with a fresh cup of hot tea and sat down on the couch. Maka lay there, doing what she always did as people approached. She stared at them as if she were a dragon and waited for them to sit down next to her before she would get up and sit in their lap. Yael knew it was about to happen and she let the cap hop up once she crossed her legs and got comfortable.

"Are you ready to hear a story?" Maka gave no reply. The cat was busy maneuvering to find the right place to sprawl her gray fur and could have cared less about Yael or her letter. She just wanted a familiar lump to lay down upon.

Yael broke open the scroll with her initials on it. It looked odd and she had no memory of seeing this colored paper before, so she opened it with caution. The seal was newly pressed and as soon as she looked at it, she could tell that she had not read its contents. Some fear crept into her heart, as she knew there would be secrets inside that he had not told her. There was a note rolled up and in the middle. She started with that.

*Yael, my dear, you know how much I love you.*
*You are the apple of my eye and I get a smile on my*
*face each time I see you read. Since you are new*

*to marriage, I thought I would give you these two stories. You can share them with Caleb once you are ready. I certainly want you two to learn from Val and me and not repeat our mistakes.*

*One day, you may find them useful during those moments when your man acts a bit stupid. If he is anything like me, you will run out of fingers and toes to count his errors before your second child comes into the world.*

His letter made her laugh as she could hear him saying it. She could hear him reprimanding her husband at the same time, calling him names yet always ending his moments with Caleb with a hug and a prayer.

"I miss you, uncle," she said as she set down the introduction and unrolled the first scroll.

She looked at the date at the top of the scroll, which indicated that this letter was more than 30 years old.

"This is older than your great grandfather, Maka," and she began to read it.

*"After a few short months in Crete, Val and I are back again in Rome. We have been here long enough to prepare to travel to Caesarea to make our new home. Val wanted to see her parents before we left and my parents agreed to meet us at their house. I am glad our families get along.*

*Now that I am back home and have time to reflect on the changes in my life, I see that my spiritual life is almost as dynamic as my professional life. It is hard to imagine that just a season ago, my mother and father blessed and sent Val and I on our first assignment together. I felt the gods' blessing as we departed, and I carried with me a small statue of Jupiter that my father gave me. I was proud to have it with us to keep us safe. Now, I don't think I will be taking it with me.*

*Our departure ceremonies were different this time as we prepared to leave for Judah. Instead of a banquet with friends and family, speeches, and blessings, my parents invited my wife and I to a small, quiet Ebreet-like synagogue outside of the Coliseum that had a yellow door. It was meant to prepare us for the people and places in our new life's timeline. Instead, my father introduced us to a unique sort of authority figure. This man had two younger assistants and none of them looked like either Romans or slaves. He blessed my father upon arrival, and I found that to be most odd, considering that the last time our family expressed spirituality, we all visited the temple of Jupiter. I whispered into Val's ear, questioning her about what was happening to my father. I was perplexed.*

*My father introduced this man as his teacher and he used the Ebreet word 'rabbi.' This teacher asked me many questions and seemed to know all about my family and my personal history. He knew my father gave me my name after the Roman hero Cornelius Skippio. He also spoke to Val and used words to imply that she was his daughter. Normally, a Roman would speak to the man if both man and wife were present. This man seemed to defy our custom. Interestingly, my wife knew how to speak to this rabbi and reciprocate his greetings in a way I didn't. While she spoke to him, I asked my father how this man knew so much about us. My father smiled and held my hand briefly, telling me it was important to listen to this man's story and not be concerned about how he knew about me.*

*Once he finished talking to Val, he shared a story with us, as it was not a personal story as I expected. The tale did not take long to share, but his words seemed about as ridiculous as hearing that ducks now dig holes in the ground instead of floating in the water. He told crazy tales of a Messiah coming to earth, dying, then resurrecting, only to disappear again. It sounded like the words of a drunk fool or something that might come from the mouth of a Caesar man seeking promotion.*

*However, I could not deny one thing. I had heard the same story from Val's father three months ago and a half-day walk from here. How can that be? It is unreasonable for those details to be identical when their sources are so distant. I asked Val if her parents had been talking to this man and she thought it unlikely. I quickly asked my father if he had been talking to Val's parents, and he said no. This didn't seem to be coincidental.*

*Both men claimed that a Messiah had already come to earth in a small town in Judah called Bethlehem. I immediately doubted this story's credibility. If he was the Messiah, why were his people group enslaved and void of power? Why did he have such a bland entry into this world if he was a Messiah and a King? Lunacy, I say.*

*I politely continued to listen as it was my responsibility to honor my elders, but this far-fetched tale did not sound legitimate. The teacher could see the doubt on my face and said that the Messiah was foretold in the ancient Ebreet scroll a thousand years ago. That claim gathered my attention, as Val's father had said the same thing.*

*Val knows the man she married. She knows I am a man seeking proof; my job as a magistrate depends on thoroughly analyzing evidence before drawing conclusions. Val asked to see these scrolls that prove what this rabbi says, looking at me for approval.*

*I nodded for her to proceed. The teacher smiled, opened his arms, and gestured in agreement. He pointed to the altar and said they were on the left side. Surprisingly, Val walked up to read them and she sounded good at them. I had not heard her read before, let alone the language of the Ebreet people!*

*She quickly went through the scrolls, talking loudly to my family and translating as fast as she read. She said that many of her childhood friends were Ebreet and she learned how to read their language during the times she attended synagogue with them. Neither my mother, father, nor I knew this about her.*

*Her scrolls said this Messiah would be rejected by his own people, spat upon, struck, and hated without cause. He would be a sacrifice for sin and would be crucified with criminals. None of those claims seemed to interest me, as many could extend those attributes to thousands of different men. However, there was one claim that she added that I asked her to read again.*

*It said that he would be born of a virgin. How is this possible? As I had not seen my wife read and translate Ebreet, I knew I could justify my unbelief with a sense of shock at her new skill. I also wondered if this was not a confusion sent upon me by Discordia, our Goddess of confusion and chaos. I wondered what might be wrong with my ability to discern truth from lies. I must conclude that there was some likelihood of credibility with this claim, and I decided that I must keep my mind open.*

*Right before we left this little synagogue, the teacher gave Val a copy of the scroll and she gave him a tithe from the wages I earned in Crete. She told me she would teach me the beginnings of this language on the boat ride to Caesarea and everyone agreed that this was a great idea. It is the language of the land that I am about to work in and live in. I was reminded of how helpful it was to speak the language of Gaul while I was there. It is hard to believe that such a good idea came from a woman.*

*We left not long after that. My father said that Emperor Caligula was losing his mind and that people around the empire were being oppressed like no time he could remember. I turned to my mother and she said that it was true. Our family, though, as citizens of Rome, were immune to most of this behavior. Certainly, I didn't see any of it in the Cretan port of Heraklion. I knew I could trust my mother's opinion of what was happening to the common man as she spent much of her days working with their wives. My father said Val and I were a blessed couple to be on the next boat out of Rome!*

*My father warned us to stay away from Rome and stay hidden amongst the Palestina, and he told me to swear not to return until we received word that Caligula had fallen. They knew I could not ignore a royal summons, but they also knew this was unlikely to come if I was the Optio in Caesarea and not the Centurion. As we prepared to leave, my father performed an ancient Ebreet ceremony, passing his blessings onto me. I thought it childish as I didn't understand any of the words he spoke, but it seemed very important to him. He sat down and asked me to place my hands under his thighs while he spoke out loud. I must honor my father, but I could not see myself doing such a thing to the next generation."*

Yael didn't look up but spoke out loud to herself. "That is too funny, considering he just did that with us a few days ago," she said. Then she returned to reading.

> *"Val wanted to travel to see her parents one last time. On that visit, her father and I spent some time with the scrolls, and he also started teaching me how to read them. He pointed out other amazing things in them that also pointed to the same Messiah. Other people in their village were also talking about this Yeshua. Regardless, it will help me study and learn this language. Fortunately, we have a very long boat ride ahead of us."*

She had been so fixated on what she had read that she had not heard her mother. Once she looked up and saw her, her mother was ready with a question.

"What did you read?" Katya asked.

"Uncle Cornelius said he could not see himself giving a blessing to his children. He certainly changed his mind, didn't he?" she said to her mother. Katya smiled and laughed.

"Good men change their minds, honey. They just need time to see that they are wrong. Just keep reading." Yael closed that scroll and opened the next one.

> *"I can't believe we have already lived in Caesarea for three months, and I have not made it a priority to write down anything that has happened. I can see that the people planning this assignment knew much more than they told me.*
>
> *This woman I married is the most surprising female I have known. She was the first to see that our assignment in Crete was to prepare me for this assignment. We feel quite safe in Judah for two reasons. I am second in command in a growing city that is rich in resources. We are also many weeks away*

*from Rome and its political instability. The stories of what is happening with Caligula and his administration are between nonsense and disgusting.*

*I am pleased to write that Val is pregnant; I am not many days removed from becoming a father. I am more excited to write that I will also be this city's centurion before our child comes. Our current centurion is a great soldier, but he is aging. He approached me last night and told me he had sent a letter to Rome, suggesting that the right decision for Rome would be to promote me to the centurion's role. He is returning to his home in Greece, where he hopes to find a quiet island and retire to his love of fishing. He also knew that the Legate in charge would be a fool not to take any other advice, considering Judah's distance from Rome.*

*I have always expected to become 'the man' one day within the Roman military, but I didn't expect to achieve this outcome so early in life. Normally, soldiers serve three times as long as I have before they are considered for any leadership position, let alone one of the top ones. Once I am officially conferred this title, I will send a letter and invite my father and mother to come to visit the new centurion in the family! I suspect my mother will be more interested in her new grandchild.*

*Val and I know that we are distant from Rome, and I have little fear of leadership usurping my authority. The city and the surroundings are not big enough to justify the placement of a full tribunal of men, so I will be the top man if I deliver to Rome their taxes and keep the peace. My current centurion told me that three upcoming capital projects would test my resolve, and he said he would tell me more once the Legate officially placed the rank upon my shoulders. I look forward to the challenge! I agree with Val. This is a good and safe assignment!*

*On our second day in Judah, I heard another story of this Messiah. I went to work the way of the docks. There was a group of fishermen there and I approached them. I asked them if they had heard a tale of this Messiah and the older one said yes and told us stories. Since I had not introduced myself yet and was not wearing my uniform, I felt that his story was credible.*

*He told one memorable tale among many. He said that Yeshua and his followers were once on the edge of the Sea of Galilee and he heard Yeshua talk to the crowd. He was far from Yeshua, but he remembered Him saying that those who make peace shall be called the sons of Adonai. He said we are blessed when people insult us, persecute us, or say false things against us.*

*This story made no sense to me. They don't sound like the words of a man they call the Messiah. It sounds like he is teaching these people not to defend themselves when they are attacked but to consider it some gift to have blades held to their faces. Perhaps I will remember that the next time a man unsheathes a blade and swings it at us, 'Roman Bastards' Ha! That will not happen.*

*At the end of the second week, Val committed us to a temporary home adjacent to a brothel at the dock. I promised her I would get rid of these brothels to make things safe for her as a mother.*

*Val continues to impress me. She has integrated with the Ebreet women who worked in that area, selling goods to the "clients" at the brothel. Val dresses now in Ebreet clothing and she says they are more comfortable than her Roman gowns and robes. Val can change her tongue between Greek,*

*Egyptian, and Ebreet, and I can't keep up with her. If there is a loving god, then he loves me through the skills of this woman.*

*It is almost absurd, but I have also found that she can assist me with my job. The stories she overhears and brings home often help me address an issue before it becomes a crime that requires my men to arrest people. Her insight has helped prevent skirmishes many times now.*

*Val and I honor the day these Ebreet call Shabbat and participate in this festival. It helps now that I can understand parts of their sacred text, the Torah. I can't imagine trying to make sense of this part of the world without understanding the contents of those five scrolls. The people treat me kindly when I am with them. The other centurions in the other cities don't share this kind of story when I meet with them. They talk about getting spat upon or attacked. I walk without weapons on Shabbat! Again, thanks to Val for allowing us to integrate with this community."*

Yael closed the second scroll.

"I need to find Val," she said. Val sat on the kitchen floor, peeling potatoes the servants had just harvested. She was humming something and looked up as Yael and Katya walked in.

"Did you know about these?" Yael asked the old woman.

"Know about what?" she asked.

"Uncle gave me two scrolls of your time together. One was from your days back in Rome before you came to Caesarea. The other was after you had spent three months here and you were pregnant with Rufus," she said.

"Oh yes, your uncle was stupid back then," she said. All the women laughed.

"I just read that he was amazed that you had common sense," she said, causing them to laugh.

"Yes, he had nearly none of it," she said. More laughter ensued.

"Unless I read this incorrectly, you played a big part in him becoming the centurion," said Yael.

Val shook her head as she finished the last potato. She handed the bowl to the servants to take outside and put it in a pot of already boiling water.

"I don't think so, Yael. He did that with his wit and willingness to work hard. What I did was keep him there. I provided him with word from the streets where no soldier would open their ears to what was happening. Most people fear Roman leadership, especially those from Israel. But a young girl wearing cheap clothes and pedaling cheap jewelry hears everything! And he needed to know everything to maintain the peace and not have his power usurped," she said.

"It worked!" Val said, raising her hands. Yael's smile reflected her fixation on what Val was trying to teach her.

"That is brilliant." Yael paused for a moment to compose her thoughts.

"In his stories, he sounds amazed that you, or any woman for that matter, had good ideas," she said.

"Little One, he changed over the years. I had to be selective in what I told him. He didn't care what fabric had just come in from Egypt, but he was very interested in the movement of boats and what they were carrying. A boatful of cotton from Thessalonica would always get his attention," she said.

"And why is that?" Yael asked.

"Cotton doesn't grow in Thessalonica," she said.

"Oh," she said. Yael nodded her head in amazement. She saw that she had much to learn to be helpful to her husband.

"From what I can tell, Corn has worked hard with Caleb to make sure Caleb listens to you more than he listened to me," she said.

Yael looked at her aunt and put her hands on her hips.

"You know, he always listens to Eliza but does not talk about her. Why is that?" Yael asked.

"I don't know, honey. At least Caleb wasn't raised biased against women like Corn was. And I know he loves you. The servants can hear you two in the mornings." Yael was embarrassed that stories of their morning sexual activities were commonplace around the house.

"Tomorrow, why don't the two of us go to the docks? Let's have you cover up like a migrant peasant and let's see what we can learn, hmm?" she asked. Yael nodded with excitement in her eyes.

"And bring your baby," she said. "Men and women don't think nursing women have much to add to the value of the world other than their vaginas and breasts. Certainly, they will not think of us as a reconnaissance team, and their tongues will be loose!" she added.

"This could be a lot of fun," said Yael.

"Oh, you just trust me, Little One. We will hear some crazy words. I will help you determine which words are lies and which are true. Perhaps we might spend a few coins in the shops while we are at it," she said, winking at her soon-to-be partner in eavesdropping.

"I am ready," said Yael, taking back her child.

Yael and Val talked about the places that they wanted to visit now that the winter season was upon them. Yael returned to an earlier thought.

"You know, now that you say these things, most of the other leaders who report to Caleb have wives, and some of them complain that their husbands don't listen to any of the advice they provide," she added.

"Maybe after I am done teaching you, you can teach them," she added.

Yael smiled from ear to ear.

"I would love that," she said.

# Chapter 16:
# To Eliza of Dor

Caleb left before sunrise the next morning to go to work. Yael got up with him to make him tea, boiled eggs, and bread, and he was grateful to walk to work on a full stomach. Once he was gone, Yael waited for the other girls to join her. They ate a light breakfast and as soon as it was over, Eliza left them to walk to the market to sort out dinner. It was her turn to cook for everyone, and she took another scroll of Cornelius to read.

"This one has me a bit nervous," she said. Everyone looked at her for a second, as she was not one to admit that she was nervous.

"What is it, Little One?" her mother asked.

"I don't know. I am about to read a copy of the letter uncle sent to Rabbi Dor long before I met either of them. I don't know what is in here, and I can't figure out how my rabbi knew uncle. Neither of them mentioned it," she said.

"Well, you are certainly brave. Go read it, and come back and tell us about it," her mother said. Before she moved, Yael needed to add something to the conversation.

"Sister, everyone knows you talk about Dor all the time. Uncle had good reason to give that to you. They are trustworthy men. Remind yourself of that," she said. Eliza paused for a moment, obviously deep in thought.

"I am changing my mind. The market can wait. If it is OK with you, I am going to sit here and read it," she said. Her mother handed her a fresh cup of hot tea and everyone settled into a place on the floor as Eliza opened the scroll with her initials and began.

*To: Dor, a young man of great promise*
*From: Cornelius, Centurion of Caesarea, by appointment of Caesar.*

"Honey, this is your Dor, correct? The one at your sister's wedding? That one?" Katya asked.

Eliza was too shocked to respond with words. She nodded her head in agreement and looked up at the ceiling. She was beginning to get emotional so she cleared her throat before continuing. She asked one of the servants for a cup of water while her emotions settled down. Katya could see her daughter's reaction and she knew Eliza needed some affirmation.

"You are a strong young woman, my daughter. Cornelius loved you, and you know he gave this to you with his heart as much as he did his head. Go ahead. Read it," she said. Eliza restarted her reading but continued without making any more eye contact with her mother.

*"Salve, Young Man!*

*You have earned a good reputation among the men. I hear that you work hard and follow orders without complaining. They say you are a great listener and show a sense of empathy, much like that of a good woman. Yet you also have the strength of a great warrior. This impressive blend of the best parts of both sexes is rare, indeed! Although I am an old man and often think I have seen everything to know, men like you convince me I am wrong. Your character gives me hope for our future.*

*You have also demonstrated teaching skills to the other men, and my Optio says that you enjoy explaining to others the deeper meaning behind the tasks you are asked to perform. He recommends that you be given a leadership rank during our next series of promotions.*

*Dor, I agree with his recommendation. This is good news for you! It is certainly within my power to extend such a promotion to you.*

*Concurrently, I know your secret. One night, Val and I were preparing to sail to Rome to greet the new emperor, as he was a boyhood friend of my son. We decided to spend the night at a quiet inn by the docks so we could be off the coast of Judah before sunrise and not disturb everyone in the house with all the bags we needed to bring with us. After all, a month in Rome is a long time!*

*I wake up early each morning, step outside with my cup of tea, and pray. As I usually do as I pray, I walk. As I traveled on the docks, I heard your song."*

Eliza looked up at her mom and spoke. She needed a moment to compose herself and start to embrace the hidden truth that this was an old letter to her teacher while he was a member of the military serving here in Caesarea. Katya could sense that her daughter was shocked and didn't know that Dor used to be in the Roman army.

"Mother, I know the song that uncle is talking of! He sings this song each morning as the birds start their songs." Her voice began to crack again from the emotion of discovery.

"Eliza, he is a good man! Don't judge yet. Keep reading," said her mother. Eliza returned to the scroll.

*"I also recognized that you were singing in Ebreet instead of Greek. I asked the guard on duty by the pier who you were and he told me.*

*I quietly walked close enough to listen to you and recognized the words you used. I then discovered that you are a follower of The Way of the risen Messiah, aren't you? Do you believe a Messiah has come, died, and risen, and His spirit now dwells among us? You were looking at sunrise to the east and singing a song to him, weren't you?*

*As you know, it is a capital offense to worship anyone other than the emperor. As a Centurion, I swore an oath to uphold the laws of Rome. This discovery impacted the recommendations my Optio gave me of you. As such, this message to you shall be much longer than you expect.*

*I am uncertain if you have heard my story. Indeed, I have told it to many people, including our emperor. Yeshua is also my Lord, and He is the source of my hope. Combining the two experiences I have of you, I will give you a more thoughtful choice of paths than anyone who has served me.*

*If you wish, I will promote you to the rank of Decurion at the beginning of next month. Your pay will double and you will get an allowance to travel back to your home twice yearly. You will have ten men under your command. I will also make you my administrative assistant during those moments I serve as a magistrate. There is much you can learn there, and I need assistance from someone competent at explaining the meaning of things to the people I judge. Your skill with words would benefit me greatly and the people I govern.*

*As a second option, you can leave the military with my blessing and recommendation. I am delivering this letter so that you have much time to ponder its contents before responding to me, as I am leaving for Jerusalem tomorrow and will be gone for a week, if not longer.*

*My wisdom for you is that you should leave the military. Leave and do not look back. Do not come back to this place or me. Go out and serve Yeshua in other ways, in other places. Do not invest your life in the hierarchy or Rome, looking for identity from military success. I assure you that you will commit acts that will make you feel great shame and feel as if you have abandoned the teachings of our Messiah with your actions.*

*Why am I saying this? It is not because of anything you did or didn't do. It is because of what I have done.*

*You see, long after I was appointed Centurion and judged to be an excellent administrator and soldier, I encountered the Holy Spirit. Many hundreds of men reported to me at that time in my life, and my wife and I had two young children. We had settled down and built a fortress at the top of a hill in Caesarea. We had made this foreign land into our home away from Rome and intended to live out our days here. I decided that it would be foolish to leave my career because of the ramblings and emotions of a short and fat man prone to drinking too much wine. Simon Peter was the most underwhelming of men who had stepped into my courtyard, yet no one had spoken more truth into my life than he had."*

"Mother, I have not heard Dor speak of any of this!" said Eliza. Her mother sensed her daughter's emotional plight, leaned over, kissed her daughter on the cheek, and softly spoke into her ear.

"Just keep reading. This letter is not evil, though you know nothing of its contents. I promise you, neither of these men has betrayed you." Eliza wiped a few tears from her eyes and continued.

*"In retrospect, I have been a part of many great crimes and committed many sins that perhaps could have been avoided had I not had dual allegiance to Rome and our Lord. In all my prayers, I repeatedly asked God to show me if I was to remain a soldier in an organization that punished, maimed, and killed with limited remorse. Our savior teaches us to live a*

*life free from the shame and curse of blind obedience to the law, yet my identity as commander of this place and the men who serve Rome did not waver, and I forced men into compliance with Roman law. I did not find peace in the words of the Messiah once he said there is no shame for those in Him.*

*I had freedom as the top leader in this land like no one else did. I yearned for the power to free all men here, but no such moment arrived. For most of my life, I was lonely. I do not wish this upon anyone, let alone a fine young man like you with much promise."*

Eliza looked up and saw Val nodding her head. Val made eye contact and smiled.

"He is telling you the truth," she said. Eliza looked back down and continued.

*"Finally, I did not hear our Lord speak to me and grant me the freedom to leave my workstation. It felt as if Yeshua wanted me to sin. Perhaps it was my habit of sinning that led me to continue. I do not know. In some moments, it felt like He wanted me to repeatedly fail at following Him, much like Simon Peter failed Him repeatedly. In fact, the most powerful stories that Fat Slob told me were of his denial of Yeshua three times in the night and his not believing in His power as he walked on the sea. Just like me, he had access to incredible power and freedom, and he failed to exercise it correctly. His story is my life song.*

*Indeed, this job I chose will be a thorn in my side until I finally get enough courage to leave the identity that comes with commanding a sector of the world. Perhaps one day, Yahweh will send me a person to whom I can relinquish governance of*

*Caesarea. I don't want to put you on a path to relive my life when you can do much better than becoming like me. Indeed, I will have to train my replacement as if it is the last act I do."*

All the women were now looking at the walls and shaking their heads in disbelief. Val spoke up first.

"He didn't hate his job as much as this letter is leading on. He hated the idea of replicating himself with another who was not a follower of The Way. In fact, I am sure his prayers brought Caleb to us," she added. Yael looked up at her aunt and smiled. Her words encouraged her.

*"Dor, I want to invite you over to my private courtyard once I return. Although I am nearly an old man, I think it will be helpful for you to hear some of my stories and what you have been considering as you review what I have said. I want to give you some circumstances to consider if you pursue a military career. Based on what my men tell me, you are a listener and leave men feeling unjudged. If you worked through our system, you would have my job. You would be required to forsake the men who love you. Instead, you would hear men, and then you would judge them.*

*You are also a healer. You know how to speak and to touch with the goal of mending. I touch men with blade, nail, and whip, making them bend to the will of Rome. If you took my job, you would replace the smiles and gratitude you now receive with anger and resentment from those you touched. It is my prayer that you do not want this.*

*Today, people come to you without fear of judgment. When they come in front of me today, it is to be judged. They are fearful of my justice. I want you to fear becoming like me.*

*Go out, Young Man! Continue to be a healer and follower of Yeshua. You aren't meant to cause damage in this world. You are meant to heal and repair those who are damaged. The world needs people like you outside of the Roman military, not in the military. The world needs people like you to address the damage done by people like me.*

*If you agree, I want to send you to visit my friends who live in Gaza. They are also members of The Way, and they will help you get started. They are wealthy merchants and give their wealth to our synagogues, and they will certainly help you build a place where you can serve the Messiah's call upon your heart.*

*I became aware that the Holy Spirit had given me the gift of prophecy during Peter's visit, but I believe I had this gift before I met Yeshua. He has given me one for you.*

*I see you standing in a facility where you are the master. It is a place where you can make people feel safe so they can heal from the damage that war has done to their souls. I see you accepting anyone who walks through your doors. I see angels above the doorway leading inside and angels in the kitchen and the gardens behind the building. I see both young and old walking through the doors and you anoint them with the truth and healing the world cannot provide. I see you with followers, but your followers are different from the followers of our Yeshua. Yeshua attracted young men with little promise. You will attract young men and young women with great promise. You will minister to them and they will minister to the world. Unfortunately, I also see the building lit up with flame, burning to the ground."*

Eliza finished the last part of the scroll, crying as she read.

"Burning to the ground? What is he talking about? The Houses of Healing?" Eliza said hysterically. Her mother spoke first.

"Not all prophecies make sense during their first reading. I see now that your teacher and your uncle were wounded and incomplete men," was all she could say. Everyone looked at Katya, wanting more, but there was nothing to say.

"All men struggle with these truths, my dear. All men," was all she could say. Eliza was overwhelmed and she lay down, using her mother's thigh as her pillow. Her mother rubbed her head and neck just as she did when she was a little girl. Eliza didn't know what to say.

"His prophecy was true," added Caleb. No one had heard him approach. Two of his lieutenants were with him, as well. They had taken their sandals off as they entered the compound and walked toward the story they were hearing with fascination.

"Which one?" asked Eliza.

"He was right in that Dor will attract young women of great promise," he said with emphasis.

"We agree," said one of the lieutenants.

"I knew Dor while he was here," said the other one.

"Really?" said Eliza, quickly rising in embarrassment that a non-family member had seen her lying down in the kitchen with the bottoms of her feet exposed. That was considered inappropriate for anyone except family.

"It was a coincidence that we arrived during the time you read that letter. Please. Don't mind us," said the lieutenant.

"Dor is my rabbi!" said Eliza.

"I think everyone from Manasseh to Judah knows that, cousin," said Caleb, and it made everyone in the kitchen laugh.

Caleb turned to leave and let his men talk. All the other women left the kitchen to begin their day's tasks, but Eliza remained, talking to one of the lieutenants the rest of the morning. They each had two cups of tea while they spoke, and Eliza heard several stories about Dor. The lieutenant listened with equal intent as he learned of the House of Healing and how Dor served refugees and helped them heal from trauma.

"Dor talked with me a lot after I first began training as an officer, as I was scared to be a part of the leadership team. My family insisted I join and he helped me with my fears. Indeed, I learned about Yeshua from him. I asked him why he was always helping people and he told me the story of the Messiah, and I believed. What I am trying to say is that Dor was also my rabbi after I came here," said the man.

"Let me introduce myself. My name is David, and my family lives right down the hill from here. I have a sister, Saphira, and remnants of my family are all over this city. May I say it is a pleasure and an honor meeting one of Dor's disciples," he said. He bowed his head to her as one of Dor's acolytes.

"David, I am a young woman, not a queen. Please, you do not need to honor me like that," she said.

"Your sister says you are a queen. She told me that the ring of the emperor's house that she wears is actually your ring," he said, nearly with a stoic tone. Eliza's head turned around and she looked for her sister so that she could get mad at her for a moment. Embarrassment replaced anger as she couldn't find Yael, and she blushed.

"My sister is the right person to own that ring. She needs it to take care of Caleb," she said, trying to diffuse the topic.

"The Centurion has shared with me much about his wife and you. He told me about how all of you met and how coming home to Yael is always the best part of the day. One day, I look forward to having a woman to look forward to coming home to." The two of them looked at each other and the moment was awkward.

"I must get back to work. It was nice to meet you. Good day," he said, turning and leaving. Once he left through the gate, Eliza turned and walked toward her sister.

"Yael, what have you been telling him, big mouth?" she asked. Despite her seriousness, everyone else laughed at her embarrassment.

"I think you just heard it all. I have talked to him two or three times, and Caleb has been here each time we have spoken. He is a good man. I guess he has a great memory," she said.

"And a great interest in finding a wife, cousin," said Caleb.

# Chapter 17:
# Val and Yael spend a day learning at the docks

"Honey, it is time. Get up," whispered Val. Yael was in bed with Caleb when Val walked in, and she shook Yael's hip to get her to start moving. Yael put on the clothing that Val gave her to wear yesterday evening and they left to go to the kitchen.

Val and Yael were on the stairs and heading to the docks before sunrise. Val wanted to be there before any morning activities had started. Val knew that many of the more meaningful conversations happened after the men on the boats came onshore and the crew had unloaded their cargo. For most, that meant breakfast time. Eliza and the house servants were left in charge of all evening meal prep again, and the two women left the compound with her son in a traditional Ebreet back sling.

Val told Yael to wear the outer robe that she wore while she was planting in the fields with the servants. It was clean and smelled fresh, but it was certainly old and appeared ready to tear the next time a nail caught it. Val wore a very specific scarf that covered her head and much of her face, and it was difficult to see that all of her hair was white and her face wrinkled. Her sandals were probably older than Yael's and looked ready to fall apart at any moment. Val engaged her as soon as they were far enough from the compound not to awaken anybody.

"Honey, before we get down the docks, you need to know what to expect. Women, slaves, and foreigners are not the same as men in the marketplace. You and I are citizens of Rome, but we cannot vote or serve in an official capacity. Our two servants are wonderful people, but Rome considers them our property. Even if we freed them, only their children can become citizens with full rights. The foreigners who come here for trade have even fewer rights than you and I do, but they must also pay taxes if they wish to enjoy the protection that the military provides." Yael had a few questions but understood that she had limited rights in the Roman world.

"Your rings give you an advantage in that you are not subject to any Roman law, and you can take any person's job with no repercussions. You could be the magistrate for a day if you wanted," her aunt said.

"You know me. I have no interest in any of those sorts of jobs," she said.

"I know, but when you are here with me, you must hide your relics and rings and act like a poor woman," she said.

"So people don't think I can do anything with what I hear them say, right?" Yael said.

"Exactly!" said her aunt. Val grabbed Yael's arms and spoke quietly.

"I have tried many strategies to make myself invisible. I have gone without bathing and I have worn dirty clothing. I have tried to sell things like day-old bread, but I find that it takes too much work to appear to have a profession. What I have found the best tactic is to sit near where the men stop and talk. I also ensure that what I am selling is valuable to them. Oranges and jewelry always seem to work. Oranges are cheap and they taste wonderful in the morning. And while men are putting food in their stomachs, they say everything," she said.

Val carried a walking stick with her, but not her normal one. The one she used at home was inlaid with gold and had a leather grip at the end. Today's stick was ordinary, making her look more like a poor old woman than the wife of the great centurion.

Once they reached the docks, Val took out ten pieces of jewelry that the son of one of their servants had made. Although the quality was that of an amateur, she promised to try and sell them for him. However, inside the breast pocket of her cloak were two beautiful brooches she no longer wore. She showed them if she knew the buyer to be serious.

Life in the port was just as Val described. Most transient men spent the night in the holds of their boats. They would get up early to use the bathroom, but Caleb had men patrolling the docks to make sure they didn't defecate in the harbor but instead used a restroom that Caleb had built at the end of each of the docks. Some men vomited from all the drinking from the night before, but the soldiers had no issues with letting that discharge into the harbor. It was fish food.

Men began unloading their goods and seeking hot food sold by street merchants who had arrived at the same time they did. Various breads and meats arrived, all freshly prepared, and the men were quick to spend a lot of money to get them. Most men had been eating salted foods on their journeys to Caesarea and were grateful for hot food despite overpaying for it all. And just as Val said, the men were all talking about what they were carrying, where they were coming from, and where they were going next. It was a logistics manifest like none that existed. Despite her age, Val memorized everything that she heard, as was her habit.

Yael was amazed to discover that they were not the lone merchants selling jewelry that day. Yael laid out her oranges and Val sat across from two other jewelers but not close enough so they could hear each other's conversation. Val obviously knew them, as she gave each of them an orange at the start of the day.

As Val had told Yael what to expect, a pair of patrolling soldiers approached them as they sat on their blankets near the main pathway leading to and from the docks. They were in uniform and had just started their shift for the day.

"Please show me your peddling permit," asked the first guard, speaking politely and authoritatively. Val pulled down the hood of her cloak and looked up at the man waiting for her paperwork.

"Ms. Valentina? Uh, I am so sorry, ma'am. You have a nice day," he said, bowing his head and ready to walk away. As he began to turn, Val spoke.

"No, no, no! You wait," she said, speaking with equal authority.

"I am to sell here and I know the rules. How much is a peddler's permit now?" she asked.

"It's the same as always. Half a copper coin for a day, three coins for a week, and a bronze coin for a month."

"Here, take this," she said, handing him a single bronze coin. The man accepted it, but he was obviously perplexed.

"Write the permit for her for the month," she said, gesturing for Yael to pull down her hood so the soldier could identify her. As she reached up to pull it down, the soldier looked at her and saw her rings and necklace.

"Oh, you are my centurion's wife! I am so sorry that I didn't recognize you two ladies. Please accept my apology," he said.

"We didn't want you to recognize us!" said Val. She quickly explained to the man that their incognito appearance helped her trade, and he quickly understood.

"Take the coin and bring me back a permit," she said. The soldier agreed. Yael was about to start talking to the men, but Val put her hand on her leg and interrupted her.

"And what is your name, soldier? You know, in case I need some help while you are on duty?" she asked. Val looked at her and nodded.

"I am Avi and this is Lincoln," said the others. Val had a routine she would use to ensure that the men remained interested in protecting her.

"So, your name means 'my father,' and yours means 'village by the lake', is that not so?" she asked. Just as Val expected, the two men immediately began telling stories about their families and hometowns. They also would mention what they missed from home and always add flavor and color to their tales to make their families proud. Val would nod, smile, and make simple comments to keep them talking, as this was her chance to get to know these two men.

As they finished their stories, the soldiers promised to give the coin to the tax collector, who would return with the permit later that day. Val reached into her bag and handed each man a small loaf of fresh bread that her servants had made. They thanked her repeatedly and promised to come by often to check on her before continuing their patrol.

"So, Little One, what did you learn?" she asked. Yael had already been told that she was going to hear that question a lot throughout the day.

"The men thought we were exempt from the law because of our husbands," said Yael. Val nodded in agreement, looking up as a group of four men walked past.

"That will not be the last time you hear that. It is a great benefit to us. What else did you learn? There was a bigger lesson there." she said. Yael paused a moment before answering.

"I believe the men liked hearing you talk about their names," said Yael, speaking as if she had just discovered something valuable on the ground.

"That is right! Men will always open their mouths to talk about their names and families. Get them to talk about those two things first, and they will talk about everything else later. I have always found that if you engage a man about his name, be it Greek, Egyptian, or Ebreet, he will open his mouth like a walnut opens in wintertime," she said, pinching Yael on the thigh. They giggled for a moment before Val continued.

"Now, Little One, each time those two soldiers walk by, they will look at you and speak. Once every two times, ask them a simple question about their day and just let them talk. They are not the main source of info, but they are our protection. And take off those rings and cover that necklace! Those with interesting information will not disclose it to someone who appears wealthy and powerful, and as you are showing off."

"I am not showing off!" said Yael indignantly. Nonetheless, she took off her rings and put them in her cloak's inner pocket. Once she was done, Val tapped her thigh and winked at her for doing the right thing. Yael settled into her position next to Val and let herself be mentored.

The day happened just as Val had told her it might. During the early part of the day, a hundred men came out of the lower hulls of their boats like magical beings emerging from the ground. They always seemed to walk down the docks in pairs. Most of them passed in front of the two women; most didn't look, but one younger man did, and he squatted down to look at the jewelry. Val knew to engage him.

"Hello, young man. Who is it that you are shopping for?" asked Val. Over the next few moments, Val managed to get the man to tell his story. His name was Aellius, meaning "the sun" in Latin. His father thought him to be a troublemaker and he sent him to Caesarea to sober up. He put him on the longest boat ride leaving Rome that day to ensure the delinquent was out of sight for a few months. His father had given him a lot of coins and now that he was ashore in a foreign land, he was at a loss as to what to do with all of it. He needed to stay away from home for at least three months before his father would let him back into the family.

Val managed to extract from him that Domitian's new favorite man was Julius Agricola. They had attacked and captured a part of Iberia called Caledonia, and it was proving itself to be a great source of new resources. He said that last month's official minting of new currency, Roman coin was again made with pure silver and not as dilute with nickel as it had been under Titus. They also learned that female gladiators now fought in the Coliseum and that the new emperor liked to see contests between dwarves as well. His apparent level of education convinced Val that he was a wealthier sort of customer, so she showed him a particularly nice ruby-encrusted jewel from her inner purse. After some negotiation, the man purchased it after he manipulated the price down 15% from what Val told him it cost. Val thanked the man and gave him a few oranges to eat throughout the morning.

"And what did you learn there?" Val asked Yael as the man walked away.

"I learned that the new silver coins you just received are probably worth more than the silver in our pockets," she said. Val tapped her leg twice in happiness at what Yael was learning.

"Good job," said Val.

"And I would also say that his family liked to be entertained," she added. The man spent nearly half of his words discussing the combat in the Coliseum and the chariot races in the Hippodrome. Both structures continued to draw a mixed crowd of Roman elite and peasants to watch the competition and hopefully see bloodshed. Recent remodeling at the Hippodrome allowed it to seat more than 150,000 people, and the multi-lap chariot races were advertised all over the city. Servants much like Yael used to be now worked in the Hippodrome, bringing food and wine to the Roman elite before the races started; and the emperor attended every chariot race, no matter what might be going on. The two women speculated that he probably got drunk and passed out at an event there, which led to his father throwing him on the next boat to Caesarea.

Other customers, not much different than Aellius, interacted with them throughout the morning. As it neared high noon, it was obvious that no one from last night's arrivals was left on their boats. Val and Yael packed up their jewelry and blanket. She motioned for Yael to give her a hand, and she turned towards all the ships.

"I always save this part of my reconnaissance until the end. It doesn't work when all the other sailors are on the boats," Val winked at Yael. Yael didn't know what they were about to do, so Val clarified.

"We are going to the end of the dock to learn from the deckhands. They don't get to walk away from the boats at the start of the day like the other sailors do. They always tell a different story, and they are more likely to remember who you are. That is the game we shall play," she said. Yael didn't understand Val completely, but she could sense the confidence and knew not to question her but to follow her lead.

The old woman held Yael's arm as they walked on the wooden planks that served as the main thoroughfare for all the goods that came off the boats in the harbor. Caleb had been working to get all of them replaced once every year, and they were much safer than the last time they walked here. Soon, they had walked almost the full length of the dock and were now nearly a stadia from the shore.

"Little One, the deckhands do not have permission to go ashore and have a good time like the sailors do. They must first load and unload cargo, clean the boat, and restock the supplies. They know every inch of the boat and everywhere it has been. The good news for us is that the deckhands know the most and talk the most." Just as Val predicted, the next to last boat on the dock was occupied by a single dark-skinned man who was cleaning the upper deck. She approached him and began speaking to him in Greek. She asked him if he was Egyptian. Once he nodded yes, she switched to his language. Yael watched his countenance change as the man began to smile ear to ear as he heard his native tongue.

In a few moments, Val learned that this year's cotton crop was excellent but there was a shortage of corn in Egypt. He told them about each port city they had visited during the month, and Val had a specific question about each one. This vessel's trading journey was nearly complete and it had one more port of call before it returned to Egypt. Val thanked the man tremendously and gave him a bronze coin for answering all her questions. He thanked her and asked for her name. She hesitated before she spoke.

"My name is Val. However, she is the person you need to know. She is Yael. She will be back at the docks more often than I am," Val said. Yael bowed her head, acknowledging him.

"I am sorry, but I don't speak Egyptian," was all Yael could say.

"It is OK. Most people cannot. Your grandmother here, though; she speaks perfectly," he said.

Yael looked at Val quickly, pondering whether she should correct him for calling Val her grandmother. Val winked at her and quickly spoke to the Egyptian in Greek.

"This grandmother needs to get home! I have some grandchildren to play with," she said. The Egyptian waved and laughed as they departed.

As they walked down the docks, Val translated and told Yael what he said. Once they got back on solid ground, Yael released her aunt and let her use a walking stick to continue to trip back home.

"And what did you learn there?" Val asked. The woman stopped for a moment so that Yael could answer her.

"There will be a lot of cotton clothing coming from Egypt next month," she said.

"Yes, there will! And we are going to get a great price on it," she said.

"Because?" as Yael, a bit perplexed.

"After they return, I will get notification from your husband's men that this man's boat has arrived, and you will come down and find that man and talk to him again." Yael nodded as her plan made sense.

"Auntie, I can't do that, as I don't speak Egyptian," said Yael.

"Excuses! If you see that man again, remind him of your name and the moment the old lady spoke to him in his language. He will remember!" she said. Yael agreed to try it.

"What else did you learn?" she said.

"They need corn in Egypt," she said.

"And what do you do with that knowledge?" Yael asked.

"Sell them corn?" she replied.

"No, you can't sell them corn, but who can?" Val asked her.

"The merchants who travel to Egypt, right?" she said. The light went on in her head.

"Caleb probably knows the men who travel to Egypt and he can tell them to bring corn and go right now," she said.

"Yes, and if that deckhand is telling the truth, that merchant will make a good profit and consider your husband his ally, not a Roman soldier looking for personal gain," she said.

"Val, you are a genius. Tonight, I will talk to Caleb and tell him about this. Can you come with me and listen?" she said.

"You bet!" said Val. The two generations of women did some shopping. Once they were finished, they began their long climb up the stairs to the family compound. Yael had learned something today.

# Chapter 18:
# Loose ends at the compound before Eliza returns to Gaza

It had been two weeks since Cornelius' passing and a new way of doing things on top of the hill was fast becoming normal. Just like Cornelius before him, Caleb's work schedule dictated all the other activities. As is true in all healthy Ebreet homes, the woman controlled the activities of the estate, but now Yael was the mistress in charge, not Val. Shabbat started on Sundown on Friday or as soon as Caleb got back from work, cleaned up, and changed clothing, whichever came first. Cornelius liked to keep Shabbat simple, limiting it to family and servants. Caleb and Yael opened their estate to anyone who they thought needed a place to rest and feel comfortable being themselves. His lieutenant David, his sister Saphira, and their parents were regulars at the house, as were some of their cousins who also served with David. Val continued to mentor Yael, but she did it upon request, not every hour as she used to do. Val never gave guidance to Yael during Shabbat; this was now her house, her rules, and her guests.

Thanks to Val's tutelage, Yael was considered a generous woman in the eyes of the community. On the evening of Shabbat, she never withheld the best wine or the choicest meats from her guests. Sometimes, she would invite a family that arrived in the port late in the day to come and join them for Shabbat if they looked lost or lonely. None of them knew that she was the wife of the centurion and they were often amazed that a Roman citizen could be considerate and caring for the people that they served.

"In my past, I served the emperor and his court the best wine and the best meat. Why would I not serve my neighbors the same thing? Isn't that what the Messiah taught when he said love your neighbors as yourself?" she would say as she walked around offering people food and drink. This small ministry made sense, and Eliza encouraged her to reach out to people and include them in her affairs.

Yael's clothing at the start of Shabbat was always impeccable, and her appearance was a blend of stunning and humble. Per Caleb's request, she always wore the silver crown the men from Gaza gave her and she wore her necklace outside of her robe, as it reminded him of why he fell in love with her. Caleb always offered a toast to the women of Israel who made Shabbat possible, and he never failed to kiss his wife publicly at the end of the toast. His men would always applaud him for his efforts and they, too, would kiss their wives when Caleb kissed Yael.

Val knew this time for all the women to be together was coming to an end soon. Eliza would return to the House of Healing to finish her training, and Katya and Matthew would return to Naphtali. Val loved having them around, as it filled in the void after the death of Cornelius. The following morning, Val decided all the girls needed to spend some time digging in the dirt outside. Nothing healed the soul like getting freshly tilled soil under your fingernails, and nothing felt better than a cup of cold spring water after the last of the seeds were in the ground and all the weeds were pulled up. In less than a full day, all the girls had planted a crop of spring kitchen vegetables in the garden next to the house. Val loved to see the girls work. Yael and Katya would sit baby Mishi and baby Aaron in the dirt next to each other, and the boys would play in the ground while their mothers planted and weeded. Val knew these moments would be the foundation of these young children's lives. Eliza would sing to the boys and they would laugh and scream when she would get to the parts where she would dance and move her hands in big circles. They all had lots of fun and the children would always be hungry after an afternoon in the dirt.

While the girls worked in the garden, the servants helped Val with some older projects in the kitchen that she always wanted to get done. They moved her stove closer to the door and lowered the shelving where all her plates and bowls were kept. Val's stature was diminishing, and she needed everything closer to the ground so she could reach it.

Yael was finding that the role of the wife of the centurion was engaging and fulfilling. She and her mother established a new routine that was already helping Caleb. They would take their infants to the docks every other morning, practicing the art that Val had taught them. Each evening, Val would prompt Caleb to ask his wife what she had learned that day, and she would share her stories quickly enough to keep his attention. She filtered out stories of no interest and made it a point to speak the names of the people she met that day, as that helped her remember them the next time she saw them. Caleb used some of her insight with his leadership at their morning check-ins. David was often given the job of following up on Yael's ideas since he lived nearby and could come to Caleb and report his findings easily. This made Yael feel valuable and contributed to their city's fame as a safe place to live and raise a family.

At the start of the third week, Caleb decided Eliza was ready to go back to Gaza. The time of mourning was over and Eliza agreed it was time to return to her discipleship. The morning of departure, Yael brought out the second letter from Titus that was in the basement and she set it on the kitchen table after breakfast was cleared. It had Caleb's initials on it, and Caleb decided to read it out loud. After all, what could a dead emperor do to them now? Yael sat down at the table first, as she was the most anxious of all of them.

"So all of you know, I have not read this one," Yael said. "When I saw it, I wanted to, but I have been saving it for you two!"

Caleb spoke up. "I will read this time," he said. The letter's seal had been broken many years ago, so Caleb started reading immediately.

*From Titus, Emperor of Rome, and your lifetime student.*
*To: Cornelius, the most powerful man this emperor has ever known.*

"Another secret," said Caleb. Caleb paused for a moment, feeling a rush of emotion as memories of his mentor seemed to come back to life. Once the emotion had subsided, he continued.

*"Teacher,*

*I know I sent you a message just two days ago, but I wanted to send you another message. I am not feeling well and my physicians are bleeding me every day, trying to extract the sickness from my blood. They suggested I get my affairs in order, as they do not know if I will live much longer.*

*Two nights ago, after the two Palestina teenagers, some of the senators came to the palace to discuss the opening of the grand arch in my honor. I don't know if I was filled with the Holy Spirit, but I chose to tell them of this Messiah. They seemed extremely concerned that I was going to destroy the empire by abandoning the old gods. They pleaded with me not to do this thing. As we all drank our evening wine, they asked me many questions about the source of these ideas, and the tone of their questions concerned me. These senators can be treacherous and I feared that if I told them about Eliza and her slave, they would find a way to dispose of them like spoiled milk. As such, I remained quiet and protected my sources. Indeed, that is why one of my most trusted servants is the bearer of this letter.*

*Uncle, I fear for the life of young Eliza. I was prompted to lift her in my first prayer, asking Yeshua to empower Caleb to protect Eliza and the slave girl. He has proven that he can defend them, but only to the point that he is present with them. It is during those times I am alone that I fear for them. The slave girl knows her way around treachery. Eliza does not. Hopefully, you can offer the power of your position to protect them once they return to Judah.*

*Lastly, since this may be the last time I write to you, I must extend my gratitude. I know you and your son have invested greatly in the well-being of my soul. I know you said you had a dream that the emperor would call Yeshua my Lord. I hope that is me that you had your dream of.*

*I also told Domitian that you had a dream for him. Perhaps one day he will come and ask you about it."*

Caleb smiled as he looked up at Eliza. He put his massive hand on the side of her face and smiled at her. He could tell that she was scared.

"Fortunately, Domitian is far away from us, and we have no reason to travel to see him," said Caleb, with a sense of gratitude, as he attempted to dispel his concern.

"Wait! Does anyone know what that dream is?" Eliza asked. No one did. Caleb handed Eliza the scroll so she could read it, as well.

That evening, Eliza was unsettled. Caleb asked her if she wanted to sleep with her sister, but she thought that was too awkward.

"You are husband and wife. I can't interrupt that union," Eliza said.

"Sure, you can. In that letter you talked about to the people at Ephesus, you said I must be willing to lay down my life for my wife. If I can't offer myself as a sacrifice, then what do I have to offer?" he said. Eliza kissed Caleb on the cheek, thanking him, and accepted a chance to spend the night with her sister alone on the roof.

Eliza and one of the servants got up early. Eliza packed her things using candlelight so she could be outside at sunrise. Val could not sleep, so she came outside to be with Eliza. The two of them held hands and did not speak until the sun was fully up.

"Goodbye, auntie," she said, hugging the old woman. Eliza cried as she pulled away from the widow.

"The next time you see me will be after Dor places the shawl and beads of a rabbi around my neck. I don't know when that is, but I will come right here. I will send a letter to mother and father after

I leave Dor. The Holy Spirit has already told me what I must do. I love you." Eliza quietly walked down the stairs to the stable where her horse awaited her. It was time to be courageous and prove the emperor wrong. It was time to be tough.

# Chapter 19:
# Slavers in Court

Caleb threw all his uncle's advice to the wind after a horrible fight with Yael. He intentionally came home later than usual and he isolated himself from everyone except Mishi. His wife missed him and wanted to fix things between them, but he was too anxious to treat her like anything more than a nuisance.

"I need to review a plan to capture slavers the following morning. Any miscues might cause the loss of life, and I don't want to talk about that with anyone who doesn't understand military matters," he said dismissively.

"I understand, but I want to help," Yael said.

"Thank you, but go back to the kitchen. Let me do this," he said, shooing her away with a hand gesture that he knew she hated. They didn't speak until the next morning, and he forced himself to say "goodbye" as he left at first light. Certainly, he didn't want to talk to her, for she knew that he had his priorities wrong. Among the many items that he discarded from Cornelius' teachings was the importance of fixing things in their marriage. He put Yael to the side and focused on his job, hoping to get back to her after the issue with the slavers was addressed. His sleep was restless, but he held his wife, thanking God for her.

The next day, Caleb and his men successfully captured the boats and the slavers operating them, and Caleb took his anger out on them. They all turned out to be Philistines and he was no exception to the stereotype that Ebreet hate Philistines. The Egyptians called them "sea people" since they came into the promised land not much after the Ebreet came in from wandering in the desert, and most people thought them to be from the dirty part of Crete or perhaps the poor part of the western side of Egypt. They did not seem to be happy with what the Lord had provided them, and they were often hungry to add to the lands they controlled. Caleb interrogated them after his men captured them. They made no effort to speak any Ebreet words to them, and they barely knew any Greek. Caleb tried Farsi and Egyptian, but none of the men on the two boats seemed to understand him.

They were placed in shackles and forced to stand in a line for inspection; Caleb took off his helmet and walked down the row. He looked each man in the eye as Cornelius had taught him to and tried to assess their hearts. One of them rolled his eyes and said something under his breath. Part of what they spoke sounded like an Egyptian slur, and Caleb knew the man had insulted him. Between the body language and the word choice, Caleb reacted with a much greater force than the situation warranted. Instead of striking the man with his fist, he put his gladius into the man's gut with a much stronger force than was necessary, and it came out the other side, pouring blood onto the sandy beach. Caleb threw the man onto the grass and he cut off his hand while it was in the shackles. As the man was bleeding out, he picked up his hand and threw it to some nearby dogs. Everyone watched as the dogs picked it up and fought over it. Caleb continued to walk down the line, but now he held a bloody gladius, and his heart was pulsing with hatred.

"Take these men to court. I will try them today," he said, speaking again in Egyptian, hoping they understood.

Caleb pushed Cornelius' teachings from his mind with the same force he pushed away his wife last night. Cornelius told him not to try a man the day he was abducted. He told him that men change their hearts once they spend a night in jail, but Caleb didn't care about their hearts today. He wanted to make his point as fast as possible. There would be no slave traders in Judah, and he wanted to send that message to the entire city before sunset.

As the men lined up for trial at court, the secretary of the court approached Caleb.

"Centurion, none of these men can read or write, and no one here seems to speak their language. In fact, from what I can tell, they are a family of deaf people. There was this note on their person. It is a contract," he said, and he handed it to Caleb, and he quietly read it.

> *"We agree to pay the deaf family four gold coins in exchange for one strong and young man. For a strong and young woman, we will pay three gold coins. For a strong but old man, we will pay two gold coins. For a strong but old woman, we will pay one gold coin. Payment occurs upon delivery in the harbor at Piraeus."*

The note was in Greek and was signed by a man Caleb had not heard of. He passed the note around to his lieutenants, but no one had heard the name.

"Centurion, there is no trial to be had here. The one who spoke is now dead and the others cannot speak. They cannot defend themselves and there is no one here to defend them. What should we do?"

Cornelius told him there would be days when a fair trial was impossible. He told him that these moments would be individual. The temptation would be to wait until the requirements are met but sometimes, there would be no way to meet the requirements.

"Take the men to prison for now," he said, and he went for a walk to the small prayer park that Eliza loved. His uncle said that no matter how complicated a situation was, there were none of which the Holy Spirit could not come and be a part of. During his walk, Caleb prayed.

"Yahweh, I do not know what to do. My heart is upset. I hate slavers. I hate Philistines. I hate nosy wives. I hate deafness. And I hate indecision. What do I do? Please send me someone who can help," he asked. He got to the edge of the water and stood there, listening to the waves. He kept his eyes closed. He had no idea how long he stood there but knew it was long enough for all his men to disburse. Then, he felt a warm hand on his right forearm.

"Caleb, I am sorry about last night," Yael said.

Caleb was shocked to hear his wife's voice. He turned and spoke without thinking, as he usually did.

"I just prayed for God to answer my prayers," he said. She looked at him and smiled. It was her turn to apply Val's teachings and let the silence of her sincere apology do the hard work of changing his heart. After five breaths, everything Val promised Yael would happen came to pass.

"Yael, I am the one who needs to apologize. You are trying to help and I am not listening to Uncle Cornelius as you share. I am sorry." Yael followed Val's instructions exactly as she told her to.

"This is the part of our life where you kiss me and ask me to accept your apology," Yael said, wearing the largest and most sincere smile she could. Caleb joyfully complied and he drew her into him for a heartfelt hug.

"Do you want to hear about my latest problem?" he asked. She had a clay pot with exactly two cups of tea in it. She poured each of them a cup and they sat on one of the benches.

"Tell me!" she said. Caleb took several minutes to cover the details about the slave traders and how he discovered that they were deaf. He wanted to find their leader, but he felt like he was at a dead end.

"Sounds like he is a smart slaver," she said.

"What do you mean?" he asked.

"He went through the effort to create a written contract and gave it to them. Who does that if they are doing something against Roman law? He knew that if they were captured, they would hang, as all slavers do. He created the evidence to convict them and protect himself all at once. Don't you think he knew they might get captured raiding your territory during the day?"

Caleb nodded. That made perfect sense.

"Go on," he said. Caleb was interested in what she had to say next.

"Let them capture you," she said, very matter-of-factually.

As Caleb paused, she continued her thought.

"Perhaps let him see his ship returning with a bounty. Then take the slaver. These are hired men and not real criminals. The other end of this transaction is probably not much different than the front end," she speculated. Caleb sat there, staring at his wife. Perhaps she was as intelligent as Val.

"Caleb, let me talk to their captain. I bet I can find something," she said. Caleb didn't know how she would do that, but the prisoners had shown no signs of violence or disobedience since they were captured. Plus, hers was the best idea he had heard so far today.

"Take your best shot," he said with a tone of surrender. The two of them began sharing how they missed connecting with each other and knew they should do this more often. Yael could sense she was too aggressive in her efforts to take his time during the day, but at night, he was often too tired to do much more than play with their children, eat, have sex, and fall asleep.

"Caleb, I don't know how to approach you sometimes. Please be patient with me. I think the most important lesson from our time with aunt and uncle is how to live as husband and wife. Everything I just did, I learned from Val. My mother did not teach me any of that." Yael smiled at her husband, feeling again a closeness to him that she greatly desired.

"Cornelius told me that I will never run out of chances to apologize for how I treat you unless I push you away and keep you there. He said the strongest warriors are the ones who know how to humble themselves without someone telling them to be humble." Caleb said.

"He loved you," Yael said. After a brief pause, she stood up and gestured for Caleb to stand in front of her and kiss her. Their kiss was long, and Yael knew that she was winning her husband's heart back.

"You are right. I don't know what I am talking about a lot of the time, but I want to help," said Yael. Caleb smiled.

"You are pretty smart for being a dumb slave girl. Let's go to the jail so you can speak with these men," he said. Caleb proudly held his wife's hand as he escorted her to the jail where the men were being detained. Once they reached the cell door, she checked her coin purse, took off all of her jewelry, and motioned for the jailer to open the door to the row of jail cells.

"Close the door and leave us," she said. Moments later, she yelled out for her husband to return. He came back as she was putting her necklace and rings back on.

"Their master is less than a day south of here, down the coast, in a smaller village north of Joppa. They always return at night to deliver the people they have captured."

"How did you find this out?" he asked.

"I gave the first person who spoke two gold coins. He was a young man and spoke our language," she said. Caleb chuckled at her simple yet successful plan.

"Thank you, Yael." That was all she wanted to hear.

Two days later, the slave trader was captured and publicly crucified in the harbor with a sign above him written in all languages.

"Slavers are not allowed in Caesarea. Look what happens if you do."

Two days after he died, he was taken from the cross and cast into the sea for the creatures to eat.

# Chapter 20:
# Called to Rome

Nearly three months had passed since Cornelius' death and Caleb found that nothing was settling nor routine about the job of the centurion of Caesarea. There were some unanticipated highlights that gave him a chance to feel good about his job. Yael used much of her free time to go to the basement and study, and she was quickly becoming a scholar.

He held a grand opening for a new highway that traveled from the harbor directly to Megiddo pass and down into the Galilee. Cornelius began the road nearly five years earlier and it was finally complete. His wife loved dressing up and participating in the ceremony. Caleb asked her to stand with him and read the royal decree to the crowd. Once she declared the road open for use, he released two doves as a sign of peace with the new opening. Listening to her speak to the crowd and command authority made him smile. She was a lot like Eliza in her ability to keep people's attention and focus on the impact her words were making. Once she was done, she closed the royal decree and stood with Caleb as his partner in leading Caesarea.

The additional segment of the public road brought 50 new soldiers on payroll, and he had to create schedules for the men to travel the highway's entire length to keep it safe. The Senate had distributed the good news throughout the empire and the harbor quickly filled with ships waiting to load and unload. He had already met twice with his Legionnaire to plead for a bigger budget to expand the docks and accommodate more vessels. In the interim, he and his lieutenants would go to work before dawn the day before the start of Shabbat to make sure that the work was done before the weekly holiday. He would rush home to give his wife the life he promised her, and he sometimes fell asleep as soon as dinner was over. Yael would give him a few moments of rest before she would wake him and ask him to return to Shabbat and enjoy all the new friends that she had invited to join them. His lieutenants were always included and he watched as Yael mentored many of their wives. David was still searching for a wife, and his sister Saphira was quickly becoming one of Yael's best friends.

Yet the bad parts of the job remained. Payday and holding court remained the two worst times of the week, and he was teaching all of his lieutenants to handle these events in case he was away. He hoped he would identify some other young men of promise whom he could promote, and he planned on asking his Legate what was entailed in promoting another man. Cornelius never taught him how promotion works when he was in charge; instead, he focused on training him with what is required of a centurion. In the evening, after Mishi had gone to sleep, he would call his wife, as she was the one who could see that he needed other men who could carry the load for him.

Uncle Corn didn't communicate some lessons thoroughly. Court day was one such exercise. He spent more time than he expected trying to see if the people talking to him were telling the truth or not, and he had learned not to do anything else on the days he held court other than come home and spend time with his family. There could be nothing else on his agenda when it was court day.

Payday was no longer as traumatic as the first time, but he continued to dread anyone who approached him in the moments before it was time to distribute weekly salaries. There had already been two other men like Menes and they haunted his sleep. There remained no recourse for how it made him feel when his crucifixion team would start pounding in the first spike. He felt lonely and dirty as he would listen to the dying men cry out for mercy.

Just like Cornelius told him, his salary was more than enough, and Yael never spent more than a quarter of it maintaining their estate. His hardship allowance was meant to pay for a contingent of servants and accommodate importing all of the essentials from Rome; Yael found everything they needed in the local markets, and they could give to those in need in the community. He was quickly filling the basement up with old and silver, just as Cornelius did before him. Their children would inherit perhaps more than he did from Cornelius.

As Caleb grew into the job, Yael cultivated her response to her husband's sensitivities. He sought the sensation of belonging after a day in court. She learned how good he felt when he would finish a project, and she would be the first to offer him a cup of his favorite wine when he was done. She learned he hated being interrupted in the middle of the day by a surprise visit from her, but not if she included baby Mishi when she came to his office.

At home, she, too, had discoveries within their marriage bed. Although awkward for her at first, she learned how to initiate sex with him. When she did, he became a different man. He always slept through the night without nightmares and he kept his hand on her body all night. He treated her with kindness and gentleness, and Val told her that she was more than just a good student of Greek. Caleb loved her more than ever.

Now that the days were longer, she would wake up in the morning light, and he would stare at her and hold her thick hair. As soon as she opened her eyes, he would speak to her.

"Thank you for last night" were his normal words the morning after she would initiate giving herself to him, and he always was more attentive and a better listener the morning after. Val promised her Caleb would become this way, but she wouldn't have believed it if she hadn't seen it for herself.

"Women who initiate sex have more caring and protective husbands," one older woman from the synagogue told her. She now had personal evidence that this was true. One of the older lieutenant's wives was a part of her inner circle now, and she offered wisdom much like Val.

"Don't let children or pregnancy get in the way of having a great sex life. There is nothing he wants more than you, and if you make him conclude that you feel the same way, you will have a loyal husband who dreams about coming home to you."

But she could sense that there was one hole in his life that Caleb had not discovered how to address. Cornelius was no longer waiting for him at the top of the stairs after he had a bad day. Instead of sitting with the old man, Caleb sought to recall his teachings during his quiet times, asking himself how his uncle might handle things. Yael learned to listen to him and she asked him questions as calmly as she could, hoping he would find a way through whatever it was that upset him. Sometimes, it worked; sometimes, he would hesitate to respond because he was trying to protect her.

He was learning to hand off problems to his lieutenants to solve. He had grown quite fond of David, and Yael knew that David was ready to find a wife and settle down. David did not ask Yael about Eliza, but she sometimes wondered if they would be a good couple. David had told Caleb that he wanted a wife like Yael, even after learning that she had been a victim of rape. Caleb knew that a man with a heart like David was rare, as nearly all good men wanted to marry a virgin. Yael knew David's family to be honorable, and Caleb and Yael promised to be on the lookout for a good woman for him. David had been permitted by his father to seek out a qualified wife on his own, and he would occasionally ask Caleb for his opinion of shopkeeper daughters that he met in the markets. Caleb knew that one day, David might be his replacement, and he treated him much like the way Cornelius mentored him.

Caleb created routines to account for taxes and inspections of the aqueducts and the unfinished bridges. He kept his books open for anyone in leadership, and he left the books in his office instead of bringing them home like his peers in Corinth in Thessalonica did. He allowed for open protests and openly dined with upset merchants and traders who felt they had been deceived. Yet the problem of slavery continued. He had hoped that the public crucifixions would stop things, but it slowed them at best. He did not imagine he would be desperate for help this quickly. Occasionally, he looked at his official seal and saw that it read, "Caleb, Centurion of Caesarea". It still created wonder that he had such great authority.

"When Uncle Rufus talked about Centurions when I was a young boy, I thought of them as heroes. They seemed amazing at everything they did, and I thought they did not get their clothes dirty," he told his wife.

"That image didn't last long, did it?" she said. They recalled that he was bloodied the first day he held court by the sea. Yael remembered throwing out the shirt he was wearing that day, as the blood was too dried to remove once he finally got home. Yet his dilemma had no solution.

"Yael, I have absolute authority in the port and on all the roads in and out of town. And yet I dread going to work some days," he said. For anyone seeking to do commerce, the office of the centurion was a required relationship that required maintenance. He was now a leader on the highest of stages for a man considered to be a native. Yael knew what he needed to hear.

"You are providing a good life for us. I have everything I need. But if you wish to resign and become a woodworker, I am okay with that. Mishi is young; he will never know the difference," Yael offered him.

"No. That would be disrespectful of all the work that our uncle did to prepare me. I wish these people could learn a few lessons from Exodus and stop worshipping all these false gods of money, sex, and each other's possessions. I feel like I don't need Roman law as I judge anymore. If I use the Torah, I come up with the same verdict. But I hate that the penalty for sin is death."

Yael had learned to sense when Caleb's job required him to kill someone. He would spend time sipping a cup of wine in the kitchen, watching Mishi now that he could walk. The boy would entertain him as he moved around and interacted with the children of the servants. Caleb would be quiet and polite but seldom speak.

"I hate my job," had a translation. When he said that, it meant he had to kill someone.

For a while, the crucifixions he ordered worked and all reports of slave harvesting stopped. Then people in the synagogue told him that loved ones who were supposed to be arriving for a visit or returning from an overseas trip were lost. One time, his men found a small, relatively hidden harbor a quarter day's walk south of the city and destroyed it. He hoped that would put an end to it, but that was an unrealistic expectation. There was too much money in human trafficking for it to end because one perpetrator was publicly crucified. Greed made the risk worth it.

He didn't like most of the suggestions he got, but his Legate had an idea he decided to use.

"Caleb, get on a horse and go North and South. Visit every coastal village in your district. Talk to their leaders. Ask about their involvement in the slave trade and see if they have ideas on how to stop it. They are the real losers in this. Whatever you do, don't threaten them, even if they threaten you. They have more men in their villages than you have on payroll. Get their help. Pay them for it. Thank them every time they deliver someone to you. Otherwise, there is no hope. The money in the slave trade is growing and it is too big to ignore. You need to own this problem and stop lamenting," he said.

With that, Caleb scheduled a trip North that would take him a week. He planned to visit six of the closest villages. He decided to take his fastest horse and take nothing with him other than his bow and a change of clothes. He would sleep where they offered a bed and eat the food they placed in front of him. He had recently finished his three-year budget request and needed time away from numbers and parchment. Plus, he always liked meeting new people on new soil. And he would make some time on the day he rides home to do some hunting. He missed harvesting and eating fresh game.

As his Legate got on his boat to sail to visit another centurion, he bid him farewell and began to walk home. As he walked up the stairs that evening, he remembered another one of his uncle's teachings.

"Tell your feet that you are going up to freedom and safety. Tell your soul that you are leaving the burdens of the day with the son of God. Then take the most important part of your being home to your family. Leave the baggage behind and love them as they are. Perhaps they will love you as you are."

Caleb didn't want to tell his wife about his work problems. The life of a soldier was hard enough. The life of a centurion was harder. He looked down and saw that there was blood all over his centurion's cloak. He swore, knowing his wife and aunt would see it and ask him questions about it. His lone resort was a partial truth and a request to trust him in handling the affairs in the city below. He knew they would honor it but he always hated the questions about what happened today. He knew he needed to be humble if he wanted to receive his wife's love in return, and he had long since made peace with the truth that sex was the best thing to put him to sleep. Fatigue and exhaustion were trumped by the thoughts in his mind and the memories of those he sentenced to death. Life without Yael was formally impossible.

Certainly, he didn't want another blow-up like the one he had a few months ago. They apologized but neither of them had a plan to prevent it from happening again.

Once Caleb finished climbing the steps and arrived home, he did what he always did. He kissed his wife, took Mishi in his arms, and went for a walk. Caleb would always lift him and whirl him around in a circle, tossing him into the sky, and wait for him to squeal with joy. He loved playing with his son, and his son loved the moment his father came home from work.

Their second child would soon be here, as Yael's pregnancy was now obvious. She loved her husband's greetings but knew her life was about to change. Two children is more than twice the work of one; every woman told her that. She treasured her husband's arrival as much as gold and silver. Soon, however, he would have less time with Mishi and would have to split his allegiance with their next child.

Caleb walked in and called for his servants. They took his sandals, cloak, and armor, and he quickly bathed off the day's grime at the spring that flowed onto their property. He dried off using a large towel made of Egyptian cotton and put on a clean robe and softer sandals not meant for walking on the stone streets and wooden docks below. He walked to grab Mishi but his aunt's voice distracted him. The sun would be setting soon and he wanted 'normal' to start as soon as possible.

"Caleb, come here!" Val said. It was a command, not a request. He knew that when she used that tone, the matter was important. As he approached her, he bowed his head in reverence to her as his elder, but she spoke as he lowered his head, interrupting his motion.

"A scroll from the emperor," she said, handing him the small rolled-up parchment. Indeed, it had the seal of the house of the Flavian dynasty on it. Yael was next to him, and he looked at her ring. The seal matched the pattern of his wife's ring, meaning it was authentic. For a moment, his heart stopped. This was his first letter directly from the emperor, and he had no idea what he would want from the distant province of Judah.

"Be brave, boy," she said, using words that she had heard her husband use.

His wife stepped next to him as he opened the seal and read with him. She read out loud slower than he read to himself, and he looked up long before she finished.

*To: Caleb, centurion of Caesarea, and his family.*

*From: Domitian, Emperor of Rome*

*You are requested to present your budget to the Senate and me at the next full moon. We look forward to appeasing Queen Leda and Neptune himself with our affairs. The state will provide hospitality at the villas next to our great empire's palace in the Palatine hills. We will celebrate and entertain for a week and make plans for our future conquests.*

*Commencement: 7 April*

*Completion: 13 April*

Caleb swore out loud and shook his head. Yael knew he was imitating Cornelius with his choice of vulgar language.

"Oh, I don't want to go to Rome right now! I have other problems I need to deal with," were the first words out of his mouth. He wanted to tell them about the report he received today about a missing young man. He was not yet ten years old and was last seen cleaning fish that his father had caught. He was emotionally split between heartbroken and angry that anyone could capture a boy like that and sell them into slavery.

Caleb stared out into the distance and shook his head from side to side in disbelief. He stuck his tongue out of the corner of his mouth and bit down on it. His plans for the week were formally unraveled. Yael looked up at her husband and attempted to make eye contact as she knew what was happening. This invitation triggered an old trauma that never completely left his soul. He was reliving his time as a gladiator in the Roman Coliseum, and he had spoken about it repeatedly as he lay in bed with her at night and could not sleep.

"Caleb," she said as tenderly as she could, in sadness that her husband was hurting again. Val saw what was happening and she needed to speak to him as the wife of a former centurion.

"Boy, you must go. It is your duty, and you know that your family will be at risk if you defy the emperor," Val said. She turned to Yael and gave her instructions.

"Go get parchment, a quill, sealing wax, and your husband's stamp. We need to dispatch a reply that will leave tomorrow on the first vessel going to Rome," she said.

She looked at her husband, but not for approval. She looked him in the eye so he could hear her unspoken affirmation. Her eyes spoke.

"Caleb, Mishi and I will go with you." He shook his head no.

"It is just a ceremony and a place to be seen. You and Mishi don't need to go," he said. He felt it his responsibility to downplay this event. She was there in the Coliseum with him not that many years ago, and he did not want to traumatize her with whatever twist the emperor might employ to get him to act against his wishes. He could have died on his first visit to Rome. She didn't need to see that. He would find his way back to her after the trip. It would be like another day at work; this time, though, he would be gone for a month.

Caleb watched his wife go into the basement to get the parchment and he felt his chest shake. He relived his afternoon on the floor of the Coliseum, strumming his bow, putting arrow after arrow in men he was told were his enemy, to learn after he mortally wounded them that they were his brothers. He felt paralyzed again. Yael would not be his wife today if he had chosen not to kill them. He tried to smile and remind himself that he had made the right choice, but all he could see was the look on the two men's faces as he used his hunting knife to slit their throats and watched as their lifeblood spilled onto the sand floor as 70,000 people cheered for their death.

Yael returned and Caleb wrote his response exactly as Val told him to. After a few moments, Yael called everyone for dinner. As he sat down to eat, he heard his aunt speaking to him about something else, but he didn't hear her.

"What?" was all he could say.

"You are taking her with you, aren't you?" Val said with her authoritative tone. Caleb was feeling trauma.

"What?" he repeated.

"Take your wife with you!" Val repeated, this time holding his forearm.

"No!" was all he could say, with the tone of an 8-year-old who didn't want to eat his dinner.

"Caleb, you will need her," Val said, pulling on his arm to get his attention. That effort facilitated no response.

"She knows how to help you now," said the old woman. That language broke through to him. Caleb returned to the moment and looked at the two women. He knew Val was right.

"OK. I need to rewrite the letter to the emperor," he said.

"First, you need to eat. You are not in a good mood," she said, and Caleb agreed. He filled his mouth with food as fast as possible and then he reached for Mishi, setting the boy in his lap.

"First, I need some time with Tiger," he said, tickling the little boy as the two women watched him emotionally return to a stable place. Then he set the boy back down and asked one of the servants to bring him a fresh piece of parchment and the quill with ink.

"I am rewriting my response to the emperor, telling him that you, Mishi, and I are coming to see him," Caleb told Yael.

Val was the first to speak.

"Thank you," she said.

"How long will we be gone?" Yael asked.

"Perhaps three weeks or a month," he answered.

Caleb finally looked Yael in the eye and could smile. Yael knew her husband had now committed to including her in the deepest part of his professional life. Yael felt the conversation was finished and she began chatting about the little things again.

"Don't finish that letter. I am going with you," said Eliza, standing at the doorway. The look on her face was not much different from Caleb's. She was wearing the same blend of stoicism and fear, and she was also trembling. Her trauma was just as great as Caleb's. Yet, the presence of her sister was all that Yael saw.

"Eliza!" said Yael as she jumped up and ran to the door. She hugged her sister and told her to sit and join them for dinner. However, Caleb couldn't move.

"Where did you get that?" said Caleb, obviously in shock. Eliza adjusted her phylactery and prayer shawl, looking down at her rabbinical robes.

"I returned to your home and took them from your mother's closet."

The weight of the day's emotions was already overwhelming; seeing his lifelong companion wearing his dead mother's rabbinical clothing pushed him over the top. He stood up and opened his arms, and Eliza ran and jumped into them. The two of them cried bitterly and deeply for a moment before Eliza pushed herself away.

"Caleb, my training is complete. Rabbi Dor released me. I am a rabbi now. He said I am ready to find and shepherd my flock. During Shabbat last week, he had a vision for me. He saw me finding my flock in Rome in the most unexpected of places. So, I am going with you. I have to. These visions came from Adonai. I cannot refuse. I came here to see if you would go with me."

Caleb handed her the royal decree and he watched her read it. Caleb remained mesmerized by his cousin's appearance. Eliza's features were much more stunning than his mother's, and she was as beautiful as the drawings of Cleopatra he had seen. She was wearing the elegant robes of a priest of the holy temple and Caleb was overwhelmed with wonderful memories of his dead mother. Finally, he composed himself enough to talk to Eliza.

"So, you finished? You are a rabbi now, in name and training?" he asked. She nodded yes.

Caleb continued staring at Eliza, making no effort to hide his continuous stream of tears and a huge smile. He took her hands and stared into her soul.

"My mom would be very proud of you. Her robes look good on you," he said.

Eliza burst into tears again. Caleb picked up off the ground and spun her just like he did after the gladiator battle. He then set her down and spoke with as much authority as a crying man could have.

"Eliza, you have come a long way since our school days. But are you sure you want to return to Rome?" he said.

Eliza wiped the tears from her eyes and lifted Mishi as she spoke.

"No, I don't want to go! But the Holy Spirit has told me I shall find my disciples there." She allowed herself a moment to laugh before continuing.

"Yael, the Holy Spirit told me you will be one of the most important people to my disciples," she said. Yael looked at her with curiosity. She didn't know what Eliza was talking about.

Val had been quietly listening as she made a plate of lamb and vegetables for Eliza. After she had sat the plate down, she put her hands on her hips and spoke to all of them.

"You three need to leave soon. I know you said you would send your acceptance letter to the docks tonight, but you need to leave in the next few days." All three of them made eye contact, nodding their heads in agreement with Val's suggestion.

"OK. We will leave on the morning of the third day," he told them all.

Caleb quickly inked his response and included that three adults and one child would be staying in the villas.

"Tell him that we would like a larger villa. You know, one with room for an additional three or four guests." Caleb looked at Eliza and knew that she seldom asked much of him; however, when she did ask, it meant that it was important. Eliza knew there would be others with them, and he needed to trust her instead of asking about those details right now. He wasn't ready for more guests in their Roman apartment, but he knew enough to trust Eliza.

"Please provide us with a larger villa with space for additional guests," he finished the letter. Once he was done and the letter was sealed with his seal, they gave it to their fastest servant to begin walking down the stairs to deliver it.

"Caleb, you are ready. And so are you, Yael. And you too, Eliza." Val looked at each one of them and repeated those words, awaiting an acknowledgment before going to the next. She knew they weren't ready and had not experienced enough to take on the entire Senate and a new emperor, but she and Cornelius had done all they could. It was time for the baby birds to leave the nest and fly.

The story is continued in book 5, "Follow Me."

www.ingramcontent.com/pod-product-compliance
Lightning Source LLC
Chambersburg PA
CBHW060447310726
48977CB00001B/346